Horatio Hastings Weld

The Patriot Boy and how he Became the Father of his Country

A Life of George Washington for Young Folks

Horatio Hastings Weld

The Patriot Boy and how he Became the Father of his Country
A Life of George Washington for Young Folks

ISBN/EAN: 9783337307523

Printed in Europe, USA, Canada, Australia, Japan

Cover: Foto ©Raphael Reischuk / pixelio.de

More available books at **www.hansebooks.com**

AND

HOW HE BECAME THE FATHER OF HIS COUNTRY

A

LIFE OF GEORGE WASHINGTON

FOR YOUNG FOLKS

ILLUSTRATED

BOSTON

LEE AND SHEPARD, PUBLISHERS

NEW YORK

CHARLES T. DILLINGHAM

1885

PREFACE.

E present here, for the study of our youth, the history of the Father of his Country. When Napoleon, the most illustrious monarch of the elder nations, met an American at Toulon, he inquired of him, "How fares your countryman, THE GREAT WASHINGTON?" By all sorts and conditions of men, throughout the world, his greatness and his goodness are acknowledged, and it is reasonable that we should be proud of him. He is our standard, by which we judge others who aspire to authority; he is the model, by which the honourably ambitious endeavour to shape their own characters; he is unlike all other heroes, for there is nothing in his actions or opinions to be concealed, nothing to be kept in the shade, nothing which does not tend to increase our love and admiration of him. It is very important, therefore, that everything respecting Washington should be made familiar to the people. The first word of infancy should be mother, the second, father, the third, WASHINGTON. Through life, his glorious example should be constantly before the citizen, to animate and encourage him in the performance of duty.

This little volume, written to interest and instruct the young, is from the most authentic materials. It is one of a series of works, of a similar description and purpose, which will be issued by its publishers.

CONTENTS.

CHAPTER I.

CHAPTER II.

CHAPTER III.

CHAPTER IV.

CHAPTER V.

CHAPTER VI.

CHAPTER VII.

CHAPTER XIII.

CHAPTER XIV.

CHAPTER XV.

CHAPTER XVI.

CHAPTER XVII.

LIFE

OF

GEORGE WASHINGTON.

~~~~~~~~~~~~~~~~~~~~~~~~

CHAPTER I.

GEORGE WASHINGTON was born in the parish of Washington, Westmoreland County, Virginia, on the 22d of February, 1732. He was descended from a family which first became known about the middle of the 13th century. It was then a custom in England for gentlemen to take the name of their estates, and from William de Hertburn, owner of the manor of Washington, in Durham, descended the various branches of the Washington family in England and in this country. In 1538, Lawrence Washington, Esquire, was proprietor of the manor of Sulgrave, in Northamptonshire. One of his sons was a baronet, and married to a sister of the Duke of Buck

(9)

ingham. Two others, John and Lawrence, emigrated
to Virginia, where they became successful planters.
John was the grandfather of George Washington,
whose father, Lawrence Washington, at the time
of his birth, resided near the banks of the Potomac,
but soon after removed to an estate near Fredericks-
burg, where he died, after a sudden illness, on the
12th of April, 1743, at the age of forty-nine.

Mrs. Washington, on whom the education of her
children now devolved, was a remarkable woman.
She had much good sense, tenderness and assiduity.
She had been very beautiful, and a great belle in the
northern part of Virginia. Her manners, however,
were unaffected, and she possessed all those domestic
habits which confer value on her sex. She lived
until her son reached the highest pinnacle of glory,
and it is related of her, that being at a ball given to
him, at this period, she said to him when nine o'clock
came, with perfect simplicity, " Come, George, it is
time to go home." Her fears, combined with her
affection, in his youth, prevented a measure, which,
if persevered in, would have given a direction to
the talents and views of her son, very different from
that which laid the foundation of his fame. Young
Washington, when only fifteen years old, solicited
and obtained the place of a midshipman in the Brit

ish navy; but his ardent zeal to serve his country, then at war with France and Spain, was, on the interference of his mother, for the present suspended, and for ever diverted from the sea service. She lived to see him acquire higher honours than he ever could have obtained as a naval officer; nor did she depart this life till he was elevated to the first offices, both civil and military, in the gift of his country. She was, nevertheless, from the influence of long established habits, so far from being partial to the American revolution, that she often regretted the side her son had taken in the controversy between her king and her country.

The means of education, one hundred years ago, were in this country very inferior to those which my young readers enjoy. There were no common schools, and the richest inhabitants did not, in most cases, attempt to give their children more instruction than was necessary to fit them for the discharge of ordinary business. George Washington's first teacher was a tenant of his father, named Hobby, who lived to see his pupil commander of the American armies; and he used to boast that he had " laid the foundation of his greatness." He afterwards went to the school of a Mr. Williams, where he maintained that standing among boys which he was

destined to sustain among men. Such was his character for veracity that his word was sufficient to
settle a disputed point with the scholars, who were
accustomed to receive his award with acclamations;
and such his reputation for courage as well as firmness, that though he never, on any occasion, fought
with his fellows, he never received either insult or
wrong. He was as much beloved as respected, and
when he left school, it is said that the scholars parted
from him with tears.

Washington's mother was very fond of fine horses,
insomuch that when, on one occasion, she had
become possessed of a pair of handsome greys,
she caused them to be turned out to pasture
in a meadow in front of the house, from which
they could at all times be seen from the window of
her sitting-room. It chanced that she, at one time,
owned a favourite young horse, which had never
been broken to the saddle, and no one was permitted
to ride him. On some occasion, a party of youths, on
a visit to the house, proposed, after dinner, to mount
the colt and make the circuit of the pasture. No
one could do it, and many were defeated in attempt
ing to mount, or thrown from the colt's back afterwards. George succeeded, however, and gave the
favourite such a breathing that he at length fell

under his rider, who immediately went and told his mother what he had done. Her reply deserves to be recorded. "Young man," said she, "I forgive you, because you have the courage to tell the truth at once; had you skulked away, I should have despised you."

The contemporaries of Washington have generally represented his early life as grave and thoughtful, but docile, inquisitive, and diligent. His love of military affairs was always apparent. He would form his schoolmates and other associates into companies, and with them parade, march, and fight mimic battles. There was a certain adjutant Muse, well acquainted with military tactics, who taught him the manual exercise, and loaned him the best books of that day on the art of war; and a Monsieur Van Braam instructed him in fencing. He was also very fond of all sorts of athletic sports, of running, jumping, wrestling, tossing bars, and other feats of agility and bodily exercise. These practices were continued by him, indeed, in mature life. It is related of him, that his character for judgment and sincerity was so high as to win the deference of other boys, who were accustomed to make him an arbiter in their disputes with each other, and never were dissatisfied with his decisions.

The manuscript school-books of Washington have been preserved, and they indicate the natural cast of his mind. Among them is a Book of Forms, such as notes of hand, receipts, bills of exchange, deeds, and wills, written out with his own hand, before he was fifteen years old. The most interesting of these books, however, is one called Rules of Behaviour in Company and Conversation; consisting of maxims and regulations of conduct, drawn from various sources, which he made at about the same period. It inculcates the moral virtues, strict courtesy in his social intercourse, and, above all, the practice of a perfect self-control.

Soon after he left school, Washington went to reside with his elder brother, Lawrence, at his place on the Potomac river, called Mount Vernon, in honour of the admiral of that name. Lawrence Washington had married a daughter of William Fairfax, a gentleman of great wealth and influence in the colony, who lived at Belvoir, a short distance from Mount Vernon, and with his family George now became intimate. William Fairfax was a distant relative of Lord Fairfax, an eccentric nobleman, who was at this time residing at Belvoir. Lord Fairfax was owner of one of the largest estates in America. It was between the Potomac and Rap pahannoc rivers, and stretched across the Alleghany mountains. It was unsurveyed, and settlers were beginning to select and occupy the finest parts of it. To enable him to claim rents, and give legal titles, it was necessary that the land should be divided into lots, and accurately measured. He had formed a very high opinion of Washington's abilities, and determined to intrust to him these important duties. It was in March, 1748, just a month after his sixteenth birth-day, that, with young George Fairfax, William Fairfax's eldest son, Washington set out upon his first surveying expedition. It was a most laborious and fatiguing service. The season was stormy, and still cold; the rivers were swollen by the recent rains, so as to be impassable except by swimming the horses, and the forests were pathless and trackless. But he performed his duty in such a manner as to give perfect satisfaction to his employer, and establish his professional reputation. He soon after received a commission as a public surveyor, and for three years was almost constantly engaged in this pursuit, strengthening his habits and constitution by hardships and exposures, and increasing all the while his reputation for integrity, energy, and ability.

The French, as the first European discoverers of that river, claimed all that immense region whose

waters run into the Mississippi. In pursuance of
this claim, in the year 1753, they took possession of
a tract of country supposed to be within the char-
tered limits of Virginia, and were proceeding to erect
a chain of posts from the lakes of Canada to the
river Ohio, in subserviency to their plan of connect-
ing Canada with Louisiana, and limiting the English
colonies to the east of the Alleghany mountains
The high character which Washington had gained
is shown by the fact that now, when he was not yet
twenty-one years of age, he was selected by the
royal governor of Virginia, to convey a letter to St.
Pierre, the French commandant on the Ohio, remon-
strating against the prosecution of these designs, as
hostile to the rights of England. The young envoy
was instructed to ascertain the objects of the enemy;
to conciliate the affection of the native tribes; and
to procure as much useful intelligence as possible.
In the discharge of his duty, he set out on the 15th
of November, from Will's Creek, then an extreme
frontier settlement, and pursued his course through a
vast unexplored wilderness, amid rains and snows,
over rivers of difficult passage, and among hostile
tribes of Indians. When his horses were disabled,
ne proceeded on foot, with a gun in his hand and a
pack on his back. He observed every thing with

the eye of a soldier, and particularly designated the forks of the Monongancia and Alleghany rivers (the spot where Fort Duquesne was afterwards built, and where Pittsburg now stands) as an advantageous position for a military post. Here he secured the confidence of several neighbouring Indians, and persuaded them to accompany him. With them he ascended the Alleghany river and French Creek, to a fort on the river le Bœuf, one of its western branches, where he found Le Gardeur de St. Pierre, the commandant on the Ohio, delivered to him Governor Dinwiddie's letter, and receiving his answer, returned with it to Williamsburg on the seventy-eighth day after he had received his appointment. The patience and firmness which he displayed on this occasion merited and obtained a large share of applause. A journal of the whole was published, and inspired the public with high ideas of the energies both of his body and mind. From this interesting journal, the first publication of Washington, we here present some extracts:

"I took," he says, "my necessary papers, pulled off my clothes, and tied myself up in a watch-coat. Then, with gun in hand, and pack on my back, in which were my papers and provisions, I set out with Mr. Gist. The next day, after we had passed a

B

place called Murdering Town, we fell in with a party
of French Indians who had lain in wait for us. One
of them fired at us, not fifteen steps off, but fortunately missed. We took the fellow into custody,
and kept him till nine o'clock at night, then let him
go, and walked the remaining part of the night without making any stop, that we might get the start so
far as to be out of the reach of pursuit the next day,
since we were well assured they would follow our
track as soon as it was light. The next day we
continued travelling until quite dark, and got to the
river about two miles above Shanopin. We expected
to have found the river frozen, but it was not, except
about fifty yards from the shore. The ice, I suppose, had broken up above, for it was driving in vast
quantities.

"There was no way of getting over but on a raft,
which we set about with but one poor hatchet, and
finished just after sunsetting. This was a whole
day's work. We next launched it — then went on
board and set off — but before we were half over,
we were jammed in the ice in such a manner that
we expected every moment our raft to sink, and ourselves to perish. I put out my setting-pole to try
and stop the raft, that the ice might pass by, when
the rapidity of the stream threw it with such force

WASHINGTON'S NARROW ESCAPE.   Page 19.

against the pole, that it jerked me out into ten feet water; but I fortunately saved myself by catching hold of one of the raft-logs. Notwithstanding all our efforts, we could not get to either shore, but were obliged, as we were near an island, to quit our raft and make for it.

"The cold was extremely severe, and Mr. Gist had all his fingers and some of his toes frozen. The water was shut up so hard that we found no difficulty in getting off the island the next morning on the ice, and proceeding to Mr. Frazier's. We met here with twenty warriors who were going to the southward to war; but coming to a place at the head of the Great Kenawha, where they found seven people killed and scalped, (all but one woman with light hair,) they turned about and ran back, for fear the inhabitants should rise, and take them for the authors of the murders. They report that the bodies were lying about the house, and some of them torn and eaten by the hogs. As we intended to take horses here, and it required some time to find them, I went up three miles to the Yohogany to visit Queen Allequippa, who had expressed great concern that we had passed her in going to the fort. I made her a present of a watch-coat and a bottle of rum, which atter was thought much the best present of the two."

In the midst of such wild scenes, were the first
years devoted by Washington to the service of his
country passed. It might have been expected that
this apprenticeship to savage warfare would have
made his deportment rough and his disposition fero-
cious.   But it was not so.   In the whole course of
his after-life he maintained a mild courtesy to all
mankind, and throughout his long military career
not one act of cruelty was ever laid to his charge.
His piety and principles placed him above the reach
of contamination, and neither adversity nor prosperity could corrupt his mind or influence his manners.
The gold was too pure to become rusted by any vicissitudes.

The House of Burgesses was then in session,
when he arrived at Williamsburg, and Washington
happening to enter the gallery, the speaker immediately rose, and moved that " the thanks of the House
be given to Major Washington, who now sits in the
gallery, for the gallant manner in which he executed
the important trust lately reposed in him by his excellency Governor Dinwiddie." Every member of
the House now rose and saluted Washington with
a general bow, and the sentiment of the speaker
was echoed by more than one member expressing
his sense of his merit and services. Washington in

vain attempted to make his acknowledgements for this high honour. His voice failed him, and the frame that never before or after trembled in the presence of an enemy, now faltered under the compliments of assembled friends. It was then that the speaker, noticing his embarrassment, made him this just and memorable compliment,—"Sit down, Major Washington; your modesty is alone equal to your merit." It will appear in the sequel that this modesty accompanied him through his whole life, and while it acted as a stimulus to new exertions, checked every feeling, or, at least, exhibition, of pride at their success. Though, in all probability, aware of his superiority over other men, this consciousness never operated to diminish his ardour to increase it by every means in his power; nor did he ever yield to the common foible of youth, which converts premature honours into an excuse for a total remission of all future efforts to deserve them.

The French were too intent on their favourite project of extending their empire in America, to be diverted from it by the remonstrances of a colonial governor. The answer brought by Washington induced the assembly of Virginia to raise a regiment of 300 men, to defend their frontiers and maintain the right claimed in behalf of Great Britain over the disputed territory. Of this George Washington was appointed lieutenant-colonel, and advanced with two companies, early in April, as far as the Great Meadows, where he was informed by some friendly Indians, that the French were erecting fortifications in the fork between the Alleghany and Monongahela rivers; and also, that a detachment was on its march from that place towards the Great Meadows. War had not been yet formally declared between France and England, but as neither was disposed to recede from their claims to the lands on the Ohio, it was deemed inevitable, and on the point of commencing. Several circumstances were supposed to indicate a hostile intention on the part of the advancing French detachment. Washington, under the guidance of some friendly Indians, in a dark rainy night surprised their encampment, and, after firing once. rushed in and surrounded them. The commanding officer, Mr. Jumonville, was killed, one person escaped, and all the rest immediately surrendered. Soon after this affair, Col. Fry, the chief officer, died, and the entire command devolved on Washington, who speedily collected the whole regiment at the Great Meadows. Two independent companies of reguiars, one from New York, and one from South Carolina, shortly after arrived at the same

place. Col. Washington was now at the head of
nearly 400 men. A stockade, afterwards called
Fort Necessity, was erected at the Great Meadows,
in which a small force was left, and the main body
advanced with a view of dislodging the French from
Fort Duquesne, which they had recently erected, at
the confluence of the Alleghany and Monongahela
rivers. They had not proceeded more than thirteen
miles, when they were informed by friendly Indians,
"that the French, as numerous as pigeons in the
woods, were advancing in a hostile manner towards
the English settlements, and also, that Fort Duquesne
had been recently and strongly reinforced." In this
critical situation, a council of war unanimously re-
commended a retreat to the Great Meadows, which
was effected without delay, and every exertion made
to render Fort Necessity tenable. Before the works
intended for that purpose were completed, Mons. de
Villier, with a considerable force, attacked the fort.
The assailants were covered by trees and high grass.
The Americans received them with great resolution,
and fought, some within the stockade, and others in
the surrounding ditch. Washington continued the
whole day on the outside of the fort, and conducted
the defence with the greatest coolness and intrepidity.
The engagement lasted from ten in the morning till

night, when the French commander demanded a parley, and offered terms of capitulation. His first and second proposals were rejected; and Washington would acccept of none short of the following honourable ones, which were mutually agreed upon in the course of the night. " The fort to be surrendered on condition that the garrison should march out with the honours of war, and be permitted to retain their arms and baggage, and to march unmolested into the inhabited parts of Virginia." The legislature of Virginia, impressed with a high sense of the brave and good conduct of their troops, though compelled to surrender the fort, voted their thanks to Col. Washington and the officers under his command, and they also gave three hundred pistoles to be distributed among the soldiers engaged in this action, but made no arrangements for renewing offensive operations in the remainder of the year 1754.

In the course of the next winter, orders were received, that officers who had commissions from the king, should be placed above those belonging to the province, without regard to their rank. The feeling of what was due to him as an American, prevented Washington from submitting to this unjust regulation, and he resigned his commission. Many letters were written to him, to persuade him not to do so; and he answered them, with an assurance that he would "serve willingly, when he could do so without dishonour." His eldest brother had died, and left to him a farm called Mount Vernon, situated in Virginia, near the Potomac river; he took possession of it, and began to employ himself industriously in its cultivation. While he was thus engaged, General Braddock was sent from England, to prepare and command troops for the defence of Virginia, through the summer. Hearing of the conduct of Washington as an officer, and of his reasons for giving up his commission, he invited him to become his aid-de-camp. He accepted the invitation, on condition that he might be permitted to return to his farm when the active duties of the campaign should be over. The army was formed of two regiments of British troops, and a few companies of Virginians. The third day after the march commenced, Washington was taken ill, with a violent fever. He would not consent to be left behind, and was laid in a covered wagon. He thought that it was very important to reach the frontier as soon as possible, and he knew the difficulties of the way; he therefore proposed to General Braddock, who asked his advice, to send on a part of the army, while the

other part moved slowly, with the artillery and bag-
gage-wagons. Twelve hundred men were chosen,
and General Braddock accompanied them; but
though not cumbered with baggage, their movements did not satisfy Washington. He wrote to his
brother, that, "instead of pushing on with vigour,
without minding a little rough road, they were halt-
ing to level every molehill, and erect bridges over
every brook." What seemed mountains to them,
were molehills to the ardent temper of Washington.
His illness increased so much, that the physician
said his life would be endangered by going on, and
General Braddock would not suffer him to do so,
but gave him a promise to have him brought after
him, so soon as he could bear the ride. He recovered sufficiently, in a short time, to join the advanced troops; and though very weak, entered immediately on the performance of his duties.

General Braddock proceeded on his march without
disturbance, until he arrived at the Monongahela
river, about seven miles from Fort Duquesne. As
he was preparing to cross the river, at the place
since called Braddock's Ford, a few Indians were
seen on the opposite shore, who made insulting ges-
tures, and then turned and fled as the British troops
advanced. Braddock gave orders that the Indians

should be pursued. Colonel Washington was well acquainted with the manner in which the French, assisted by Indians, made their attacks; and being aware of the danger into which the troops might be led, he earnestly entreated General Braddock not to proceed, until he should, with his Virginia rangers, search the forest. His proposal offended Braddock, who disregarded the prudent counsel, and ordered his troops to cross the river; the last of them were yet wading in it, when the bullets of an unseen enemy thinned the ranks of those who had been incautiously led into the entrance of a hollow, where the French and Indians were concealed by the thick underwood, from which they could securely fire on the English. In a few moments, the fearful war-whoop was sounded, and the French and Indians rushed from their shelter on the astonished troops of Braddock, and pursued them to the banks of the Monongahela.

In vain did their commander, and the undaunted Washington, endeavour to restore them to order and prevent their flight. The deadly aim of the enemy was so sure, that in a very short time Washington was the only aid of General Braddock that was left to carry his orders and assist in encouraging the affrighted troops. For three hours, he was ex-

posed to the aim of the most perfect marksmen;
two horses fell under him; a third was wounded;
four balls pierced his coat, and several grazed his
sword; every other officer was either killed or
wounded, and he alone remained unhurt. The Indians directed the flight of their arrows towards his
breast, and the French made him a mark for their
rifles; but both were harmless, for the shield of his
God protected him, and "covered his head in the
heat of battle." His safety in the midst of such
attacks, astonished his savage enemies, and they
called him "The Spirit-protected man, who would
be a chief of nations, for he could not die in battle."
Thus did even the savages own a divine power in
his preservation; and the physician, who was on the
battle-ground, in speaking of him afterwards, said,
"I expected every moment to see him fall;—his
duty, his situation, exposed him to every danger;
nothing but the superintending care of Providence
could have saved him from the fate of all around
him." This battle took place on the 8th of July,
1755. In a note to a sermon preached a month
afterwards, by the Rev. Mr. Davies, of Virginia, we
find mention made by the author of " that heroic
youth, Colonel Washington, whom I cannot but hope

BRADDOCK'S DEFEAT. Page 28.

Providence has hitherto preserved, in so signal a manner, for some important service to his country.".

General Braddock was mortally wounded, and his few remaining soldiers then fled in every direction. But his brave and faithful aid, with about thirty courageous Virginians, remained on the field, to save their wounded commander from the hatchet and the scalping-knife of the Indians. They conveyed him with tenderness and speed towards that part of his army which was slowly advancing with the baggage, and he died in their camp, and was buried in the middle of a road, that his grave might be concealed from the Indians by wagon-tracks.

In writing an account of this dreadful defeat, Washington said, " See the wondrous works of Providence, and the uncertainty of human things!" He was much distressed by the loss of the army; and the officer next in command to General Braddock, instead of endeavouring to prepare for a better defence, went into winter-quarters, although it was only the month of August. It was thought necessary to raise more troops immediately, and the command of all that should be raised in Virginia was offered to Washington, with the privilege of naming his own officers. He willingly accepted this offer, as he could do so witnout placing himself under British

commanders, who were not really above him in rank.
He immediately set off to visit the troops that had
been placed in different situations along the borders
of the province; and on his return to prepare for
an active defence, he was overtaken by a messenger
with an account, that a number of French troops
and Indian warriors, divided into parties, were cap-
turing and murdering the inhabitants of the back set
tlements, burning the houses, and destroying the
crops; and that the troops stationed there, were unable to protect them. Washington immediately used
every means within his power to provide for their
relief; but it was impossible to defend, with a few
troops, a frontier of almost four hundred miles, from
an enemy that " skulked by day, and plundered by
night." While he was anxiously doing what he
could, he wrote to the governor an account of the
distress around him; and added, " I see their situation, I know their danger, and participate in their sufferings, without having the power to give them further relief than uncertain promises. The supplicat-
ing tears of the women, and the moving petitions of
the men, melt me with deadly sorrow." It might
have been expected, that the people in their distress
would blame him for not protecting them better; but
no murmur rose against him; they all acknowledged,

that he was doing as much for them as was within
his power. He wrote the most pressing requests for
more assistance; but instead of receiving it, he was
treated unkindly, as he related in a letter to a friend.
" Whence it arises, or why, I am truly ignorant,
but my strongest representations of matters, relative
to the peace of the frontiers, are disregarded as idle
and frivolous; my propositions and measures as partial and selfish; and all my sincerest endeavours for
the service of my country, perverted to the worst
purposes. My orders are dark, doubtful and uncertain. To-day approved, to-morrow condemned; left
to act and proceed at hazard, and blamed without
the benefit of defence. However, I am determined
to bear up some time longer, in the hope of better
regulations." Though disappointed in all his best
formed plans, by the obstinacy and ill-nature of the
person who had the power to control him, and pained
by the increasing sufferings around him, which he
was not enabled to relieve, yet he did not suffer an
angry resentment to induce him to give up the effort
of doing some good. He continued his active and
humane endeavours, and pleaded for the relief of
his suffering countrymen, until his pleadings were
called impertinent. In answer to this he wrote to
the governor, " I must beg leave, in justification of

my own conduct, to observe that it is with pleasure I receive reproof, when reproof is due; because no person can be readier to accuse me than I am to acknowledge an error, when I have committed it; or more desirous of atoning for a crime, when I am sensible of being guilty of one. But on the other hand, it is with concern I remark, that my conduct, although I have uniformly studied to make it as unexceptionable as I could, does not appear to you in a favourable light." With calm dignity he endured a continuance of such vexations, without ceasing to toil in his almost hopeless work of humanity.

A new commander of the British troops was sent from England, and he listened to Washington's opinion, that the frontiers could not be freed from the attacks of the Indians, in connection with the French, until they were driven from Fort Duquesne; for that was the place from which they started on their destructive expeditions. When it was determined that this should be attempted, Washington advanced with a few troops, to open the way for the army; but before they reached the fort, the French left it. The English took possession of it in November, 1758, and named it Fort Pitt. As Washington had expected, the possession of this fort prevented all further attacks on the frontiers; and when his countrymen were secured from the dangers against which he had left his farm to assist in defending them, he determined on returning to it. His health had been injured by his exposure to se- .ere cold, and being often, for many days, unsheltered from the falling rain; and he felt that he ought to use means to restore it, as he could do so without neglecting a more important duty. He resigned his commission, and the officers whom he had commanded united in offering to him affectionate assurances of regret for the loss of "such an excellent commander, such a sincere friend, and so affable a companion."

Soon after his return to his farm, in the twenty-seventh year of his age, he married Mrs. Custis, a lady to whom he had been long attached, and who was deserving of his affection. She had an amiable temper, and was an agreeable companion; and in performing all the duties of a wife, she made his home a scene of domestic comfort, which he felt no desire to leave. Employing himself in directing the cultivation of his ground, and in the performance of all the private duties of his situation, he lived for several years in retirement, except when attending the legislature of Virginia, of which he was a member.

For the benefit of his health, he sometimes visited

a public spring in his native state, to which sick persons went, with the hope of being relieved by using the water. At the season when there were many persons there, it was the custom of a baker to furnish a particular kind of bread, for those who could afford to pay a good price for it. One day it was observed by a visiter, that several miserably poor sick persons tottered into the room where the bread was kept, and looked at the baker, who nodded his head, and each one took up a loaf, and, with a cheerful countenance, walked feebly away. The visiter praised the baker for his charitable conduct, in letting those have his bread, whom he knew could never pay him; but he honestly answered, " I lose nothing. Colonel Washington is here, and all the sick poor may have as much of my bread as they can eat; he pays the bill, and I assure you it is no small one."

Such was the beginning of the career of the greatest of men. This book is prepared for the youth of our country. Let them remember while they read it, that it was *goodness* as well as energy and ability which made our Washington's the first name in the world. In these days it is needful for all to study his character, and emulate it, that the republic of which he was the FATHER, may not be riven and destroyed.

CHAPTER II.

SOON after the peace of Paris, 1763, a new system for governing the British colonies, was adopted. One abridgment of their accustomed liberties followed another in such rapid succession, that in the short space of twelve years they had nothing left they could call their own. The British parliament, in which they were not represented, and over which they had no control, both claimed and exercised the power of taxing them at pleasure, and of binding them in all cases.

Claims so opposed to the spirit of the British constitution, and which made such invidious distinctions between subjects residing on different sides of the Atlantic, excited a serious alarm among the colonists. Detached as they were from each other by local residence, and unconnected in their several legislatures, a sense of common danger made apparent to them the wisdom and propriety of forming a new representative body, composed of delegates from each colony, to take care of their common interests.

With very little previous concert, such a body was formed and met in Philadelphia, in September, 1774, and entered into the consideration of the grievances under which the people laboured. To this congress Virginia deputed seven of her most respectable citizens: Peyton Randolph, Richard Henry Lee, George Washington, Patrick Henry, Richard Bland, Benjamin Harrison, and Edmund Pendleton; men who would have done honour to any age or country. They were appointed in like manner to attend a second congress on the 10th of May, in the following year. The historians of the revolution will detail with pride the proceedings of this assembly: the firmness with which they stated their grievances, and petitioned for redress; the eloquence with which they appealed to the people of Great Britain, the inhabitants of Canada, and their own constituents; the judicious measures they adopted for cementing union at home, and procuring friends abroad. They will also state the unsuccessful termination of all plans proposed for preserving the union of the empire, and that Great Britain, proceeding from one oppression to another, threw the colonies out of her protection, made war upon them, and carried it on with a view to their subjugation. All these matters, together with the commencement of hostilities at Lexington, and the formation of an American army by the colony of Massachusetts, for defending themselves against a royal army in Boston must here be passed over. Our business is only with George Washington. The fame he had acquired as commander of the Virginia forces, together with his well-known military talents, procured for him the distinguishing appellation of the Soldier of America. Those who, before the commencement of hostilities, looked forward to war as the probable consequence of the disputes between Great Britain and her colonies, anticipated his appointment to the supreme command of the forces of his native country.

An incident illustrative of his religious habits at this period of his life, is preserved on unquestinoable authority. During the session of Congress, a gentleman, residing in the city of Philadelphia, anxious to learn the chief of the strangers who had assembled from the several colonies, observed to Mr. Secretary Thompson, that he had heard much of Mr. Washington from Virginia, and would be glad to know how he could distinguish him. Mr. Thompson replied, " You can easily distinguish him when Congress goes to prayers—" *Mr. Washington is the gentleman who kneels down.*" Thus, in the prime of life, did he, who was as noted for his modesty as for his merit, manifest to the world his sense of the overruling providence of God.

As long as he continued a member of Congress, he was chairman of every committee appointed to make arrangements for defence. These duties were soon superseded by more active employment in the field. As soon as Congress had determined on making a common cause with Massachusetts, against which a British army had commenced hostilities, they appointed, by an unanimous vote, George Washington, commander-in-chief of all the forces raised or to be raised for the defence of the colonies. His election was accompanied with no competition. The same general impulse on the public mind, which led the colonies to agree in many other particulars, pointed to him as the most proper person for presiding over their armies.

To the president of Congress announcing this appointment, General Washington replied in the following words:

"Mr. President,

"Though I am truly sensible of the high honour done me in this appointment, yet I feel great distress from a consciousness that my abilities and military experience may not be equal to the extensive and important trust. However, as the Congress desire it, I will enter upon the momentous duty, and exert every power I possess in their service, and for support of the glorious cause. I beg they will accept my most cordial thanks, for this distinguished testimony of their approbation.

"But lest some unlucky event should happen unfavourable to my reputation, I beg it may be remembered by every gentleman in the room, that I this day declare with the utmost sincerity, I do not think myself equal to the command I am honoured with.

"As to pay, sir, I beg leave to assure the Congress that as no pecuniary consideration could have tempted me to accept this arduous employment, at the expense of my domestic ease and happiness, I do not wish to make any profit from it. I will keep an exact account of my expenses; those I doubt not they will discharge, and that is all I desire."

A special commission was made out for him, and at the same time an unanimous resolution was adopted by Congress, "that they would maintain and assist him, and adhere to him with their lives and fortunes, for the maintenance and preservation of American Liberty."

He immediately entered on the duties of his high station. After passing a few days in New York, and making some arrangements with Gen. Schuyler, who commanded there, he proceeded to Cambridge, which was the head-quarters of the American army. On his way thither, he received from private persons and public bodies, the most flattering attention, and the strongest expressions of determination to support him. He received an address from the Provincial Congress of New York, in which, after expressing their approbation of his elevation to command, they say, "We have the fullest assurances, that whenever this important contest shall be decided by that fondest wish of each American soul, an accommodation with our mother country, you will cheerfully resign the important deposit committed into your hands, and reassume the character of our worthiest citizen." The General, after declaring his gratitude for the respect shown him, added, "Be assured that every exertion of my worthy colleagues and myself, will be extended to the re-establishment of peace and harmony between the mother country and these colonies. As to the fatal, but necessary operations of war, when we assumed the soldier we did not lay aside the citizen, and we shall most sincerely rejoice with you in that happy hour, when the reestablishment of American liberty, on the most firm and solid foundations, shall enable us to return to our private stations, in the bosom of a free, peaceful, and happy country."

A committee from the Massachusetts Congress received him at Springfield, about one hundred miles from Boston, and conducted him to the army. He was soon after addressed by the Congress of that colony in the most affectionate manner. In his answer, he said, " Gentlemen, your kind congratulations on my appointment and arrival, demand my warmest acknowledgments, and will ever be retained in grateful remembrance. In exchanging the enjoyments of domestic life for the duties of my present honourable, but arduous station, I only emulate the virtue and public spirit of the whole province of Massachusetts, which, with a firmness and patriotism without example, has sacrificed all the comforts of social and political life in support of the rights of mankind, and the welfare of our common country. My highest ambition is to be the happy instrument of vindicating these rights, and to see this devoted province again restored to peace, liberty and safety." When Gen. Washington arrived at Cambridge he was received with the joyful acclamations of the American army. At the head of his troops, he published a declaration previously drawn up by Congress, in the nature of a manifesto, setting forth the reasons for taking up arms. In this, after enumerating various grievances of the colonies, and vindicating them from a premeditated design of establishing independent states, it was added, "In our own native land, in defence of the freedom which is our birthright, and which we never enjoyed till the late violation of it; for the protection of our property, acquired solely by the industry of our forefathers and ourselves, against violence actually offered; we have taken up arms: we shall lay them down when hostilities shall cease on the part of the aggressors, and all danger of their being renewed shall be removed, and not before."

When Washington joined the army he found the British strongly entrenched on Bunker Hill. The American army had been assembled from different colonies. It was without discipline, and was composed of most discordant materials. He commenced immediately the difficult task of bringing the men into proper order. Their hands, which had been only used to felling trees, striking the anvil, guiding the plough, or to other peaceful and useful employments, could not readily handle well a musket or a sword. They knew nothing of the discipline that

was needful to make them good soldiers. They
resolved to defend their rights, but this spirit of freedom caused them to wish to do so in their own way,
and as they were not willing to submit to rules and
directions, the patience of their commander was
often severely tried. He had naturally a strong
temper, but in his boyhood he had determined to
watch and subdue it. When any occurrence raised
his anger, he resolutely endeavoured to restrain it.
He knew that he could not command others so as
to have their respect, if by the indulgence of pas-
sion he proved that he could not command himself.
In addition to the difficulty of regulating the army,
he had the anxiety of knowing that they were very
scantily supplied with powder and arms, as there
was very little powder in the country, and the inhabitants of the different provinces did not wish to
part with what they thought they might want to use
for their own particular defence. Washington was
very anxious to conceal this deficiency from the English generals, and used every means possible to do
so. His army was placed so as to blockade the English troops, who were stationed on Bunker's Hill,
Roxbury Neck, and in Boston. Knowing as he did
the difficulty there would be in getting supplies for
his men, he wished to make an attempt to drive the

enemy from Boston at once; but his officers on being consulted, were of the opinion that the attempt would not be successful, and the two armies continued in the same situation for several months.

As it was known that the English were endeavouring to engage the inhabitants of Canada, and the Indians, to assist them in invading the provinces from that part of the country, Congress sent troops there, who took possession of several forts. Washington resolved to send a detachment from his army to Quebec, and he gave the command of it to Colonel Arnold. The orders given to him were, to pass through the country, not as an enemy to the inhabitants of Canada, but as friends, and to check with severity every attempt to injure them; and to treat with respect their religious ceremonies: for, said Washington, " while we are contending for our own liberty, we should be very cautious of violating the rights of conscience in others, and should ever consider, with a true Christian spirit, that God alone is the judge of the hearts of men, and to him only in this case are they answerable." Arnold and his troops were thirty-two days passing through a frightful wilderness, without seeing a house or a human being; they waded through swamps and toiled over mountains, and arrived at Quebec worn down with

READING THE DECLARATION.   Page 42.

fatigue. Arnold expected to take Quebec by surprise, but information had been given of his approach, so that he was disappointed. General Montgomery, who had taken Montreal from the English, marched to join Arnold, and then endeavoured to prevail on the commander of Quebec to give it up without blood being shed; but the officer he sent with a flag of truce was fired on, and he then determined on attacking the town. The attack was bold but not successful, and in making it the brave Montgomery lost his life. The blockade of Quebec was continued for some time without effect, and, on hearing that an English fleet had arrived, the American officers concluded that it would be vain to expect success, and gave up the siege. Several engagements convinced the Americans that their force was not sufficient to accomplish in Canada what they had expected; and the officers determined on retreating from it, before their men should be more reduced by unavailing sufferings.

At the time of these occurrences in the north, the southern provinces were not quiet. The governor of Virginia, assisted by ships of war, attempted to burn the town of Hampton, but he was prevented by the bravery of the people. He then collected his force at Norfolk. An American regiment of regulars, and two hundred minute men, marched for the defence of that place; they were attacked by the English, whom they soon forced to retreat, with the loss of many of their number, though the Americans did not lose one man. The governor took refuge on board of a vessel; and on the night of the first of January, 1776, a heavy cannonade was commenced on the town from the ships, and some of the troops landed and set fire to the houses. As the Americans did not think that they could keep possession of Norfolk against the force of an English fleet, they made no efforts to extinguish the flames, but suffered them to rage until the town was consumed. After this the governor continued sailing up the rivers of Virginia for some time, burning houses and destroying plantations. A number of the inhabitants of the frontiers of the southern provinces, were inclined to favour the English, and formed themselves into companies; but they were met by the provincial parties, and obliged to fly in every direction. The governor of North Carolina had gone aboard of a ship of war in the Cape Fear river. General Clinton, who was to command the English in the south, arrived in North Carolina, with a small force; but he did not think it prudent to use 't there, and determined on going to Charleston, in

South Carolina. This intention was discovered, and all ranks of citizens began immediately to prepare for defence. A new fort, afterwards called Fort Moultrie, in honour of its commander, was quickly built on Sullivan's Island, which is at the mouth of the harbour. In the beginning of June, the British fleet anchored off the harbour of Charleston. Some American troops arrived from Virginia and North Carolina, and they were all commanded by General Lee. The streets of the city were barricaded; store-houses of great value were pulled down, and every possible means for defence were prepared. The English fleet was commanded by Sir Peter Parker, and consisted of two fifty-gun ships, four frigates, and four smaller armed vessels. On the 28th of June, they commenced firing on Fort Moultrie, at about 10 o'clock in the morning, and continued to do so for three hours; but the firing was returned from the fort with so much skill, that the ships were almost torn to pieces, and about 9 o'clock, with difficulty were moved off. The loss of the British in killed and wounded, exceeded two hundred; while that of the Americans was only ten killed and twenty-two wounded.

Thus did a feeble force of 375 regulars, and a few militia, in a half-finished fort, defeat, with little loss to themselves, a powerful and well-commanded fleet. A few days afterwards, all the English troops who had been landed, returned to the vessels, and the whole fleet sailed away for New York; and the state of South Carolina was, for that time, delivered from the ravages of a foreign army.

This success given the Americans in the south, encouraged them greatly, and cheered the anxious mind of Washington, when he was distressed by the unfavourable accounts from the north. His army had been very much changed during the winter; many of the men had returned to their homes, and new recruits had taken their places; so that he was constantly obliged to bear the trial of patience in his endeavour to have a regular force. He was still of opinion, that an attempt to drive the enemy from Boston would be successful; in writing to Congress on the subject, he said, " I cannot.help acknowledging, that I have many disagreeable sensations on account of my situation; for to have the eyes of the whole continent fixed on me, with anxious expectation of hearing of some great event, and to be restrained in every military operation, for want of the necessary means to carry it on, is not very pleasing; especially as the means used to conceal my weak-

The Battle of Sullivan's Island. Page 46.

ness from the enemy conceal it also from our friends and add to their wonder."

Towards the latter end of February, having received a fresh supply of powder, he resolved on attempting to force General Howe from Boston, and commenced an attack early in March; a considerable detachment of Americans took possession of the heights of Dorchester, and in one night, though the ground was frozen, raised works, which in a great degree covered them from the shot of the enemy. It was then necessary for the English, either to drive the Americans from those heights, or to leave the town; the former was determined on, and troops were put on board of the ships to proceed down the bay for that purpose. They were not, however, allowed to succeed, for they were scattered by a violent storm, and entirely disabled from proceeding; and before they could be ready again to make the attempt, the Americans had made their works of defence so strong, that it was thought useless to try to force them. In expectation that most of the troops would be engaged in this attack, General Washington had made preparations for attacking those that remained in Boston; but this plan was disappointed by the English general determining on leaving it, when he saw that the Dorchester heights

E

could not be taken. When General Washington knew
of the intentions of General Howe, he thought it
most probable that he would go from Boston to New
York, and therefore sent a large portion of his army
there immediately.

On the 17th of March the English entered their
ships, and soon the whole fleet sailed. The rest of
the American army then marched to New York.
The recovery of Boston caused great joy. When
Washington entered it, he was received by the inhabitants as their deliverer from oppression; and in
their public address to him, they expressed the wish
he might " still go on, approved by Heaven, and re-
vered by all good men." The fleet sailed to Hali-
fax, remained there until June, then left it, and early
in July landed the troops on Staten Island.

CHAPTER III.

HE revolutionary war afforded few very striking events compared with those of some European contests. It was a long and arduous struggle, between her feeble colonies and the most powerful of nations, in which only the greatest genius, guided by patriotism, and supported by the public enthusiasm, could have triumphed.

On the evacuation of Boston, by the British, General Washington immediately left his position at Cambridge, for New York, where, after many difficulties, he arrived in the month of April, 1776. There he received a letter from the President of Congress conveying the thanks of that body to himself and his army, for their conduct at the siege of Boston. He replied with his usual modest manliness—"I beg you," he says, "to assure them, that it will ever be my highest ambition to approve myself a faithful servant of the public; and that to be

in any degree instrumental in procuring for my
American brethren a restitution of their just rights
and privileges will constitute my chief happiness."
Speaking of having communicated the thanks of
Congress to the army, he adds, " They were indeed
at first a band of undisciplined husbandmen, but it
is, under God, to their bravery and attention to their
duty, that I am indebted for that success which has
procured me the only reward I wish to receive, the
affection and esteem of my countrymen."

He found New York ill-prepared for defence in
the event of General Howe's directing his operations
to that quarter. The state troops were deficient in
arms, and many of the citizens as much so in
patriotism. Owing to various causes, the tory influence was strong in that quarter. A considerable
number of British troops were always stationed in
New York; the officers had many of them inter-
married with the most influential families of the
province; and a number of the proprietors of the
largest estates were devoted loyalists. Add to this,
the Asia, man-of-war, lay opposite the city for some
time, having it entirely at her mercy, and the commander threatening destruction in case of any overt
act of opposition to the royal government.

These and other causes damped the efforts of the

whigs, and delayed decisive measures of defence. But the body of the people finally obtained the ascendency over their disaffected opponents, and aided by a body of troops from Connecticut, under General Lee, maintained possession of the city in defiance of the threats of the commander of the Asia. That officer declared that if any troops came into the city, he would set it on fire; and Lee replied, " that if he set fire to a single house in consequence of his coming, he would chain a hundred tories together by the neck, and make that house their funeral pile."

The possession of New York, the key to the Hudson, which forms the geographical line of separation between New England and the South, and is, moreover, the most direct route to and from Canada, was deemed an object of the first importance. Accordingly, Washington used his utmost efforts to place it in the best possible state of defence. At his recommendation, Congress authorized the construction of such a number of rafts calculated to act as a sort of fire-ships, armed boats, row-galleys, and floating batteries, as were deemed necessary to the command of the port and river. They likewise voted the employment of thirteen thousand militia, to reinforce the main army under Washington.

Until now the Americans had been contending for

their rights as subjects of England; but the time had arrived when the contest was to assume a different character. An event was at hand which was to change the relations between the mother country and her colonies, and separate their future destinies for ever. The assertion of rights had produced the desire of independence. To the more sagacious of that great and illustrious body of men which composed the first Congress, it gradually became evident that, though the ancient relations of the two countries might perhaps be revived for a time, there never could in future subsist that cordiality which was indispensable to their mutual interests and happiness. Blood had been shed; bitter invectives and biting insults had been exchanged; injuries never to be forgotten, and outrages not to be forgiven, had been suffered; and the filial piety of the children had been turned into hatred of the tyranny of the parent.

They saw, too, that were England to relinquish her claim to parliamentary supremacy for the present, there would be no security for the future. The colonies would be left as before, equally exposed to a revival and enforcement of the obnoxious claim of taxation without representation. Union could no longer subsist compatibly with the mutual happiness

of the two parties, and a separation became the only
security against eternal family strife. The lofty
pride of patriotism, which disdains to wear the yoke
even of those we have been accustomed to reverence, when it presses too heavily, came in aid of
these considerations, and enforced the only just and
rational conclusions.

Actuated by these motives, on the 7th of June,
1776, Richard Henry Lee moved in Congress that
a declaration of independence should be adopted.
Three days after the question was postponed to the
first of July; but in the mean time, Thomas Jeffer-
son, John Adams, Benjamin Franklin, Roger Sher-
man, and Robert R. Livingston, were appointed a
committee to draft the proposed declaration. The
day being come, the subject was taken up, the declaration read, and the most important question that
ever arose in this country settled for ever, by the
adoption of that Declaration of Independence which
has become the political law of all who love and
strive for the maintenance or recovery of their
rights.

Soon after Independence was declared, the brother
of General Howe arrived at Staten Island, with a
large fleet, and a number of regiments. General
Washington had made preparations for defending

New York; but was convinced that he could not prevent the English ships from passing up the Hudson. While he was busily engaged, letters were sent from the commander of the fleet, to the governors under the king, requesting them to make known to the people that he had authority to grant pardons to all who would return to their duty; and that every person who would aid in persuading them to do so, snould be rewarded. Washington sent these papers immediately to Congress, who resolved to publish them. At the same time, General Howe sent an officer with a flag of truce, and a letter addressed to "George Washington, Esquire." He refused to receive it, as he considered it a disrespect to his countrymen, who had given him the title of "Commander-in-chief" of their armies. Another letter was sent, directed to George Washington, &c. &c. &c., and the officer who brought it said that the addition of "&c. &c. &c." meant every thing that ought to follow the name. Washington said "they meant every thing, it was true, but they also might mean any thing;" and he would not receive a letter on public business, if directed to him as a private person. The officer assured him no disrespect was intended, and that General Howe and his brother had been appointed by the king to "settle the un happy dispute which had arisen." Washington told him that he had no power from Congress to say any thing on that subject; but, from what he could learn, it was his opinion that General Howe and his brother were authorized only to grant pardons, and " those who had committed no fault, wanted no pardon."

The English army consisted of about twenty-four thousand men; it was abundantly supplied with military stores, and a numerous fleet was ready to aid it. The American army, of about thirteen thousand men, for three different situations, was poorly armed. Washington endeavoured to encourage his troops; he said, " the time is perhaps near at hand, which will determine whether Americans are to be freemen. The fate of unknown millions will depend, under God, on the courage and conduct of this army. Let us rely on the goodness of our cause, and the aid of the Supreme Being, in whose hands victory is, to animate and encourage us to great and noble actions."

General Howe landed on Long Island on the 22d July, and Washington prepared for an attack; a detachment which had been stationed to give notice of the approach of the enemy, was surrounded and captured; and this gave the English an advantage

in their assault, which was made with so large
a force, and in so many different directions, that
it was not in the power of the Americans to
resist with success, though they did so with bravery Washington passed over to Brooklyn, and
saw, with regret, the destruction of his troops. He
had no power to aid them in any other way than by
his own exertions; for he saw that if he brought
over the rest of his troops from New York, the superior force of the enemy would overpower them all,
and thus the fate of the country at once be decided.
The English encamped in front of the remaining
Americans, and Washington determined on an effort
to save them by a withdrawal from Long Island. He
formed his plan, and when the night of the twenty-
eighth came, all the troops and military stores, with
a great part of the provisions, and all the artillery.
were carried over to New York in safety. Providence
favoured the Americans with a night so dark, and a
morning so foggy, that though their enemies were
within a few hundred yards of them, they did not
know of the movement which was being made, until
they were beyond the reach of their guns. From
the commencement of the action, on the morning
of the 27th of July, until the troops had crossed

safely, on the 29th, their commander had not slept
He did not think of his own preservation until the
last boat was leaving the shore, when he placed himself in it, with a sad spirit. The affair of Long
Island discouraged the Americans so much, that
Washington had to suffer the pain of seeing
whole regiments return in despair to their homes.

From the movements of the English, Washington
found it was their intention to surround New York,
and force him into a battle. The depressed state
of the army convinced. him that this would be dis-
astrous, and he determined to withdraw toward
Philadelphia.

When the American troops left the city, they proceeded to the upper part of the island, and the enemy
immediately afterward took possession. Lord Howe
followed up his advantage by opening a negotiation
for peace. General Sullivan, who had been made
prisoner at the battle, was sent on his parole to Philadelphia, with a message desiring a conference on
the part of the British commander with some of the
members of Congress, as he could not treat with it
as a body. After some hesitation this proposal was
acceded to, and Franklin, Adams, and Rutledge deputed to receive the communication alluded to in

the message of General Sullivan. Without entering
on the particulars of the conference, it will be sufficient to say that it proved entirely abortive. The
republicans refused to be pardoned, and the royalist
general having nothing else to offer, expressed his
regrets, and ended the discussion.

CHAPTER IV.

AFTER the evacuation of New York which became indispensable in consequence of the operations of the British, on the 15th of September, Washington withdrew to Kingsbridge, a few miles above the city, and soon after to White Plains, where a slight engagement took place, in which a portion of the Americans were driven from their station. He then changed his position for another, and Howe, thinking this too strong to be attacked with prudence, retreated down North River, with a view to invest Fort Washington, on York Island, which, being only an embankment of earth, was surrendered after a sharp but short resistance, with three thousand prisoners. Our army was thus rapidly diminishing, while that of the royalists had been increased by a reinforcement of five thousand Hessians and Waldeckers Wash-

ington marched his forces over into New Jersey, leav
ing the British entire masters in New York. Terror
and dismay overspread the whole country. The
tories every day grew more bold and insolent; the
whigs began to despair of their cause; the neutrals
turned partisans against their country, and the enemy
became arrogant with success.

After vainly attempting to oppose the English, now
commanded by Cornwallis, at Brunswick, Washington retreated to Trenton, where he determined to
remain till the last moment, having first passed his
stores to the other side of the Delaware, in Pennsylvania. He wished to accustom his troops to the
sight of the enemy, and hoped that in the boldness
of success, Cornwallis might afford him an opportunity of striking a blow. At this time his cavalry
consisted of a single corps of Connecticut militia;
he was almost destitute of artillery; and his army
amounted to but three thousand men. One third
of these were New Jersey militia, and the time of
many of the others was about to expire. Supported
and animated by a sense of justice, however, a hand-
ful of barefooted soldiers, marching on the frozen
ground of an American winter, and tracked by their
enemies by their blood on the snow, was soon to
astonish the country by its achievements.

General Howe now issued a proclamation, offering pardon to all who, within sixty days, appeared before officers of his appointment, and signified their submission to the royal authority. Despairing of the cause, or perhaps secretly disaffected, many availed themselves of his amnesty, and an opinion prevailed among all classes, that a longer contest for independence was hopeless and impossible. But Washington never despaired. While in the full tide of retreat, General Reed is said to have exclaimed, "My God! General Washington, how long shall we fly?" "Why, sir," replied Washington, "we will retreat, if necessary, over every river of our country, and then over the mountains, where I will make a last stand against the enemies of my country."

Cornwallis remained inactive at Brunswick, leaving Washington a few days of leisure, which he employed with his usual industry in making preparations for the ensuing campaign. He urged congress, as well as the governors of the different states, by every motive of patriotism, to take measures for the safety of the country, and the success of its cause; and, while stimulating others, himself set the example which he commended.

The citizens embodied themselves with alacrity, and fifteen hundred joined him at Trenton. Thus reinforced, he moved in a direction towards the enemy, then at Brunswick. On his way, however, learning that Cornwallis was advancing by different routes with a view to gain his rear, and cut him off from the Delaware, he changed his purpose and crossed to the west side of the river, so opportunely that the enemy came in sight at the moment.

The two armies now remained opposite each other on the different banks. The object of Cornwallis was to cross over, and either force Washington to fight, or, if he retreated, to gain possession of Philadelphia; while that of Washington was to prevent the enemy from crossing the Delaware. While thus situated, General Charles Lee, who had been repeatedly urged by Washington to join him as speedily as possible, imprudently slept in a farmhouse at a distance of three miles from his command, and about twenty miles from the enemy. Information of this was given, and an English officer sent, with a company, well mounted, who reached the house and surrounded it before General Lee was awake. He was carried to the English camp, and considered as a deserter from the British service. General Sullivan, the next in command, immediately hastened the march of the troops and soon joined General Washington. All the attempts of the English to get boats to cross the river failed, and their general determined to place them in quarters for the winter, which had commenced. Some were placed in Princeton, and the rest at the principal towns of that part of New Jersey.

The invading army, to use the words of Washington, was increasing like a snowball, by the arrival of new reinforcements and the accession of the disaffected, while his own was inferior in numbers, and, as usual, deficient in all the necessary requisites for efficient action. The ice would soon form in the Delaware, and the British general might avail himself of it to cross the river and take possession of Philadelphia, for there was no force capable of preventing him. Such an event, by further depressing the lingering hopes of the patriots, would increase the obstacles to recruiting his army, now almost insurmountable.

When Washington reflected on the dispersed situation of the English troops, he said, " Now is the time to clip their wings." Urged on by the necessity of striking a blow that might awaken the energies, and revive the hopes of his country, he formed the design of attacking the enemy at the moment he was lulled in the lap of security, waiting for the freezing of the river.

E

'The design was executed, so far as the elements would permit, with success. The night was dark as pitch; the north-east wind whistled along the shores of the Delaware, laden with freezing sleet and the broken ice came crashing down the stream in masses that, as they encountered the rocks above, shivered into fragments, with a noise that might be heard for many miles. Neither man nor beast was out that night, and the enemy on the opposite shore sought shelter in the houses of the citizens of Trenton from the storm. But Washington was active. In the dead of the night, the boats were launched on the river, and after incredible exertions they reached the opposite shore. Without waiting a moment to learn the fate of the other two divisions, which were to co-operate in this daring adventure, he pressed forward towards the foe, and the dawn saw him before Trenton. The guard had no time to fire, so impetuous and unexpected was the attack; they retreated to where Colonel Ralle, the English commander, had drawn up his men. That officer soon fell mortally wounded, and his troops retreated. Washington advanced upon them, throwing at the same time a detachment in their front, when, seeing themselves surrounded, they laid down their arms, and surrendered at discretion. A thousand prisoners, with their arms, and six field-pieces, were captured on this occasion, with the loss of two Americans frozen to death, two killed, and a single officer wounded—James Monroe, who afterwards succeeded Washington as President of the republic for whose liberties they were there contending together.

The divisions of the American army which were commanded by Generals Irvine and Cadwallader, had not been able to cross the river amid the driving ice; and as that part of the plan which they were to perform failed, Washington concluded it would not be prudent to remain with his small force where he should probably be soon attacked by the collected force of his enemies; he therefore crossed the Delaware with his prisoners, and the military stores he had taken.

This bold and successful action occasioned great astonishment in the English army, as they had believed the Americans to be in a condition too feeble to attempt resistance, even when it should suit their enemies to leave their comfortable quarters to attack them. Cornwallis had gone to New York, but he returned immediately to New Jersey, to regain the ground which had been thus unexpectedly lost.

Washington resolved not to remain idle, and he passed over the river to endeavour to recover at least a part of New Jersey. The English assembled at Princeton, and formed there some works of defence. Washington collected all his troops at Trenton. The next day the English approached. He then crossed the Assumpink creek, which runs through the town, and drew up his army beside it. The enemy attempted to cross it, but were prevented, and they halted and kindled their night-fires.

The situation of Washington became very critical. If he remained inactive, he was confident of being attacked, at the dawn of day, by a force far superior to his own ; he thought the destruction of his little army must be the consequence ; and to pass the Delaware was almost impracticable from masses of drifting ice.

In this situation he resolved once more to baffle the enemy by becoming the assailant. The van of the troops under Cornwallis had taken possession of Trenton, and the two armies had nothing but the Assumpink, a stream scarcely thirty yards wide, between them. Tradition has preserved the story that Sir William Erskine urged Cornwallis to an immediate attack. It is thus related by Mr. Paulding :

" Now is the time," said he, " to make sure of Washington."

" Our troops are hungry and tired," replied the

other. "He and his tatterdamalions are now in my power. They cannot escape to-night, for the ice of the Delaware will neither bear their weight, nor admit of the passage of boats. To-morrow, at break of day, I will attack them, and the rising sun shall see the end of rebellion."

"My lord," replied Sir William, "Washington will not be there at daybreak to-morrow."

The rising sun saw Washington at Princeton, and the British at Trenton heard the echoes of his cannon amid the frosts of the wintry morning. After replenishing his fires to deceive the enemy, he had departed with his usual quiet celerity, and marched upon Princeton, where three British regiments were posted in fancied security, not dreaming of his approach. Though surprised, the enemy made a gallant defence, and he who had so long and so often been the shield of his country, now became its sword. His capacious and unerring mind again saw that another moment had come, on which hung the destinies of his beloved country. The cause of freedom was on the brink of a precipice, from which, if it fell, it might never rise again.

The British force was met in full march towards Trenton. On perceiving the advanced guard of the Americans, they faced about, and repassing a small stream, advanced under cover of a wood. A short but sharp action ensued ; the militia soon fled, and the small body of regulars, being far overmatched, was broken. At this critical moment, Washington came up with the corps under his command, and renewed the action. Seeing at a glance that all was now at stake, and would be lost by defeat, he became inspired with that spirit which always most animates courage and genius in the hour of peril. He snatched a standard, and calling on his soldiers to come to the rescue, dashed into the midst of the enemy. Animated by his words, and still more by his example, they backed him bravely. The British cried, " God save the king," and the republicans shouted, " God save George Washington." After a severe contest the British broke and fled. One hundred and twenty killed, and three hundred prisoners, were lost by the enemy, and the Americans lost sixty-three. The name of General Mercer, who fell early in the action, is alone bequeathed to posterity. An officer writing an account of the battle, said, " I would wish to say a few words respecting the actions of that truly great man, General Washington, but it is not in my power to convey any just ideas of him. I shall never forget what I felt when I saw him brave all the dangers of the field, his important life hanging as it were by a single thread, with a thousand deaths flying around him. I thought not of myself. He is surely Heaven's peculiar care."

The British troops at Trenton had been under arms, and about to attack the Americans' by the early dawn ; but when it came, they discovered that the whole force, with their baggage and stores, had withdrawn ; and they soon heard the sound of their cannon at Princeton, which, though in the midst of winter, they supposed to be thunder.

The unexpected and successful attacks made at Trenton and Princeton, by an army that was thought to be conquered, saved Philadelphia for that winter ; and revived the spirits of the Americans so much, that the difficulty of raising troops for the next season was lessened in all the states.

In compliance with the advice of Washington. Congress had resolved to enlist soldiers who would consent to serve while the war continued. When the American army had retreated through New Jersey, the inhabitants were so sure of destruction, that they thought it would be useless to make any attempt to defend themselves ; but after these successes they collected in large companies, and the militia became very active in assisting to confine the English to Amboy and New Brunswick, where they were

stationed when Washington led his army to Morristown.

During the season of deep gloom which had overspread the United States, when the hearts of all
were tried, he who bore the greatest responsibility,
felt most keenly the position of affairs. Governor
Brooks of Massachusetts, then an aid to Washington, came to him from a tour of duty in his own
state. He found him deeply affected, and as he
talked of the condition of his troops, and of the
country, he shed tears. "Sir," said he, "my hope
is in God only. Go back to Massachusetts, and do
what you can to raise men and money." From the
midst of darkness came a light that cheered all
hearts. The drooping spirits of the nation were
revived.

While the Americans were in Morristown, their
number was so small, that it was difficult to keep up
the appearance of an army; but Washington sent
out small detachments to show themselves in different directions; and with the assistance of the New
Jersey militia he succeeded in keeping the enemy
from again overspreading the country. As the
spring advanced, and new troops were raised, there
was a difficulty in assembling them as he wished,
for the English had possession of the sea; they

WASHINGTON CROSSING THE DELAWARE. Page 72.

could attack any part of the Union ; and each state desired to be defended. This could not be done, without separating the troops into small divisions, and placing them at a distance from each other. Washington was able to make the best use of small means; and he determined to prepare in the surest manner for defending the eastern states, the highlands of New York—where it was very important to preserve the forts—and Philadelphia, the possession of which seemed to be the object of Cornwallis When he had arranged troops for this purpose, he formed his own camp at Middlebrook, in New Jersey, with not quite six thousand men.

Early in June, the English army was increased by arrivals from New York, and the commander marched them in different directions, for the purpose of drawing Washington from his camp; but he was too wise to be led into the field, which would have been the scene of almost certain destruction to his small army. He continued watching the movements of the enemy with anxiety. Sometimes they appeared as if intending to go to the north, and then moved towards the south. He kept his troops in front of his camp, always ready for an attack. He wrote to General Arnold his opinion, that it was the intention of the enemy to get possession of Philadelphia, but that if they moved, he would follow after, and do every thing in his power to delay them.

General Howe, finding that he could not draw Washington from his camp, determined on taking his army on board of the fleet to the Chesapeake or Delaware. Washington took advantage of this by following the enemy cautiously. They had passed over to Staten Island, but their commander suddenly resolved on returning to get possession of the situation Washington left, but he immediately moved back, and prevented the success of this plan. The whole English army then crossed to Staten Island, and went on board the fleet.

CHAPTER V.

THE campaign of 1777 opened gloomily. A better spirit had indeed been awakened by the admirable generalship of Washington, and the confidence in his ability and patriotism had become more deep and universal. But his army was inefficient in numbers and discipline, and was wretchedly provided with clothing, arms, and munitions. At the same time Burgoyne, in high spirits, was advancing with ten thousand men from Canada, and Howe, with twice that number, was preparing for an attack on Philadelphia.

At this period the young and gallant Lafayette—whose name was destined to become the second only in two continents — first associated himself with Washington. In August, General Howe landed at the mouth of Elk River, at the head of Chesapeake Bay, and proceeded without interruption to the Brandywine. Here Washington determined to make an

effort to save the capital of Pennsylvania. The
consequence was a defeat of our army, which retreated, and was followed by the enemy, who succeeded in taking possession of the city. Lafayette
shed his first blood on the banks of the Brandywine,
and there first wrote his name in history.

The possession of Philadelphia was not to be
easily or quietly maintained. Various reinforcements placed Washington at the head of nearly as
large an army as that of Howe, toward whom he
determined to act at once offensively. A large portion of the British force was in Philadelphia, whence
the line of encampment extended through German-
town, a long straggling village, consisting principally
of stone houses, stretching on either side of the
road for nearly two miles. In this situation, it appeared to Washington that so much of the enemy
as was at this village, might be surprised and cut off,
and he promptly resolved on the undertaking. At
seven in the evening of the 4th of October, the
Americans moved from their encampment, and just
at the dawn of the morning, a division under General Sullivan encountered and drove in the outposts
of the enemy. Sullivan was quickly followed by the
main body, which immediately entered into action,
but it was more than half an hour before the left

WASHINGTON AND LAFAYETTE. Page 75.

wing came up. Each of these parties was successful in breaking the enemy; but Lieutenant-Colonel
Mulgrave, with a small body of British, having taken
possession of the strong stone edifice, known as
Chew's House, annoyed the Americans so much by
his fire that they stopped to dislodge him. The time
lost in this attempt, which was unsuccessful at last,
was a serious disadvantage. The ground, too, was
difficult, and the obscurity of the morning prevented
Washington from seeing distinctly what was going
forward. The united action of the different parties
was broken; the delay in attacking the stone house,
and various accidents, impeded the attack. The
enemy rallied, and became the assailants. The brigade under General Greene, after a sharp encounter,
was broken; the right wing faltered; the division
of Wayne, in falling back on its friends, was mis-
taken for the enemy, and confusion became general. Washington, perceiving that all hope of success was lost for that time, yielded to the disappointment of his hopes, and retired from the field about
twenty miles, and halted at Perkiomen Creek, where,
receiving a fresh reinforcement, he turned, and resumed his former position in the vicinity of the city

The fleet which landed General Howe and his
army at the head of the Chesapeake, had afterwards

entered the capes of Delaware, and sailed up that river for the purpose of aiding the operations of the land forces.

The army under the command of Washington, though directed with skill and courage, was insufficient to produce any but partial and temporary successes. Inferior in numbers and in discipline, his triumphs consisted in delaying the operations of the enemy, rather than preparing the way for his own. That, during successive years of defensive war, under every circumstance of discouragement, he saved his army and the country from ruin, was more honourable than gaining victories and conquering nations with-superior means.

In the mean time the war raged furiously in the north and in the south. The Green Mountaineers, seizing their rifles, rallied in defence of their coun try. The first check given to the triumphant Burgoyne was by the militia of Vermont. On the heights of Bennington, the Hessians were to feel the power of undisciplined freemen, unconquerable in the righteousness of their cause.

At Bennington, Breymen and Baum, two officers who had been despatched to procure supplies of cattle and horses, and to capture or destroy a stock of provisions collected by the Americans, were met by

the gallant Starke of New Hampshire. Baum, fail-
ing in his first objects, fortified himself in a favourable position, and waited for his associate Breymen.
Before he had time to arrive, the Green Mountain
Boys rushed upon his entrenchments with such im-
petuosity that nothing could stand before them. On
the first assault the Canadians fled in disorder; Baum
received a mortal wound, and not a man of all his
regiment escaped. Unknowing his fate, Colonel
Breymen came up soon afterwards, and met his vic-
torious enemies instead of his friends. His troops,
after sustaining a few fires, broke into disorder, and
sought shelter in the woods, where they were within
a short period nearly all taken.

About the same time that the parties of Baum and
Breymen were destroyed, the force co-operating with
Burgoyne, under Colonel St. Leger, consisting of
British and Indians, being met by a fierce resistance,
and alarmed by a false report, raised the siege of
Fort Stanwix, an important position on the Mohawk.
The Indians, discouraged by a tedious series of ap-
proaches, which resulted in a total disappointment
of anticipated plunder, deserted their allies; while
General Gates, who commanded the American force
in the north, was daily reinforced by brave men from
the adjoining country. Arnold, who afterwards be

came infamous by his treason, was there; and Morgan, whose better fame is equally immortal, was present with his unerring riflemen. The approach of Burgoyne from the north was connected with the expected movement of Sir Henry Clinton, with a force from the south. They were to meet at Albany. But one never arrived there, and the other went against his will, since he was carried as a prisoner.

After much hard fighting, in which Arnold, and Morgan, and Dearborn, and Brooks, and others, distinguished themselves, on the morning of the 17th of October, in the year 1777, was seen at the outlet of Saratoga Lake, the first British army laying down its arms to the Americans, who were thus not only relieved of the presence of a formidable foe, but placed in possession of a fine train of artillery, seven thousand stand of arms, and a large quantity of military stores.

This great event, it was thought, would check the advance of Sir Henry Clinton up the Hudson, and relieve General Gates of all apprehensions from that quarter. It was therefore resolved to reinforce Washington by drawing detachments from the northern army. He accordingly deputed Alexander Hamilton, then acting as his aid, to urge General Gates to a speedy compliance with the orders of

Congress. Hamilton states in a letter to Washington, that Gates discovered much unwillingness to diminish his force, and urged his apprehensions of an attack from Clinton, as a pretext for declining to furnish the required reinforcements. There are, however, strong reasons for believing that an intrigue had been set on foot to displace Washington from the command, and elect General Gates in his stead. The capture of Burgoyne had raised the reputation of Gates higher than that of any other man except Washington, if, indeed, he was an exception; and a small party was formed in Congress, aided by a few officers, not altogether destitute of claims to distinction, to place him in the chief command.

How far Gates himself participated in this project, cannot easily be decided. Happily for the country, the intrigue proved abortive. The army under Washington, the people, and even the soldiers of General Gates, rejected the idea of a change. Gates received the command of the force destined to act against Lord Cornwallis in the south, where his success did not justify the anticipations of his friends or of his enemies.

The event gave a new phase to affairs in England, and the contest began to excite deep interest on the continent. It was of importance to the states to

F

gain aid from abroad, and the prospects of success were now so greatly increased, that European powers began to seek their own advantage in forming friendly relations with our country.

When the victory was known in Pennsylvania, some of the officers of the army were so elated by it, that they were anxious to make an immediate attack on the enemy in Philadelphia. Many, who only looked on while their countrymen were toiling, thought that they knew better than Washington how to conduct the war, and were forward to express their opinions on the subject.

But Washington knew well the condition of both parties. His mind was not dazzled by the idea of the praise he would acquire by success, and he persevered in resisting public clamour, while he knew that by yielding to it he should endanger the general interests. His unyielding virtue saved the army for more important services. He was always in the best state for meeting an attack; but was resolved not to commence one.

Intelligence was brought to him that the enemy in the city were preparing to march out of it, and that it was the design of General Howe to drive him beyond the mountains. This information was given by a woman named Lydia Darrah, who resided in

Second street, opposite to General Howe's nead-
quarters, in Philadelphia. Two of the British officers selected a chamber in her house, as a secure
place in which to hold private conversations; on the
second of December they told her they would be there
at seven o'clock, and remain late; and they desired
that she and all her family would retire early. She
thought something important to the Americans was
to be discussed, placed herself in a situation to hear
what was said, and understood from the conversation that all the British troops were to march in the
evening of the fourth, and surprise Washington in
his camp. Supposing it to be in her power to save
the lives of hundreds of her countrymen, she determined to carry this intelligence to Washington.
She told her family she would go to the mill at
Frankford, where she obtained her flour; and she
had no difficulty in getting permission from General
Howe to pass the lines for that purpose. Leaving her
bag at the mill, she hastened to the American camp,
and met an officer, named Craig, whom she knew.
To him she told the secret, and made him promise
not to betray her, as her life might in that case be
taken by the British. Craig flew to Washington
with the information, and the courageous matron
returned to the city.

General Howe marched at the appointed time, but found Washington expecting him; and, disappointed, he encamped within three miles of the Americans.

A day passed, in which small detachments from each army attacked each other, and then all remained again at rest. Another day was spent in the same manner, and Washington employed himself in giving directions to every division of the army, and in encouraging all to resist with bravery. General Howe suddenly broke up his camp, and marched his troops back to the city, showing that he feared too much the result of a contest, when the Americans were in a favourable situation for meeting him.

CHAPTER VI.

N the winter following the events already related, the American army was stationed at Valley Forge, near Philadelphia. The hardships endured by the troops were almost incredible. Poorly fed, and nearly destitute of clothing, it required a confidence in their leader, and a devotion to their country, which have few parallels in history, to keep them together. It is no cause of wonder that some of them were discontented; that in their sufferings they pined for the comfortable homes which they had quitted for the battle-fields of freedom. But the great majority were firm, enduring every privation with patience and hope. Washington continued to urge on the attention of Congress the sufferings of his poor soldiers. With all the energy of true feeling, and with a manly confidence in his own claims to be heard and respected, he exhorted the legislature to remedy the defects of the commissary department, where these wants principa.ly originated, and, with the boldness of truth, lays the blame where it ought to rest. " I declare," said he, in one of his letters--" I declare, that no man, in my opinion, ever had his measures more impeded than I have, by every department of the army. Since the month of July we have had no assistance from the quartermaster-general ; and to want of assistance from this department the commissary-general charges great part of his deficiency. To this I may add, that notwith. standing it is a standing order, often repeated, that the troops shall always have two days' rations in advance, that they may be ready at any sudden call, yet scarcely any opportunity has ever offered of taking advantage of the enemy that has not been either entirely thwarted, or greatly obstructed, on that account."

During the darkest period of the encampment at Valley Forge, Washington received a letter from the English governor of New York, enclosing a resolution of Parliament to propose a reconciliation to the Americans. Offers of pardon were made, but no acknowledgment of independence. The governor requested Washington to make the resolution known to his army. He, however, sent the letter and paper tc Congress, expressing his surprise at the " extraordinary request of the governor." Congress immediately resolved to refuse accepting any offers from the English government, until the independence of the country was acknowledged. Washington enclosed this resolution to the English governor, and requested him to make it known to his army.

To show the determination of Congress on this point, and the spirit of devotion in which they had acted, it may be mentioned that Mr. Laurens, the President of that body, stated, in reply to a letter to him on the subject, that it would be unnatural to suppose their minds less firm than " when, destitute of all foreign aid, and even without expectation of an alliance ; when, upon a day of general fasting and humiliation, in their houses of worship, and in the presence of God, they resolved to hold no treaty with Great Britain unless they shall acknowledge the independence of these states."

Several letters were addressed to members of Congress, by commissioners of the British government, assuring them of honours and rewards if they would procure a reconciliation. A proposal was made to Joseph Reed, a member from Pennsylvania, that he should have the best office in America, under the king, and ten thousand pounds, if he could bring Congress to consent to the offers of the British. He replied that he was " not worth buying; but, such as he was, the king of England was not rich enough to do it." The commissioners persisted for some time in their tampering.· They sent addresses to persons of every description throughout the country, with offers of pardon, and threatenings of vengeance, but their promises and menaces were alike disregarded.

The inhabitants of the surrounding country, knowing the condition of the army, were alarmed; one of them left his home one day, and, as he was passing thoughtfully the edge of a wood near the camp, heard low sounds of a voice. He paused to listen, and, looking between the trunks of the large trees, saw Washington engaged in prayer. He passed quietly on, that he might not disturb him; and, on returning home, told his family he knew the Americans would succeed, for their leader did not trust in his own strength, but sought aid from the Hearer of prayer, who promised in his word, " Call upon me in the day of trouble; I will deliver thee, and thou shalt glorify me." Many, who, in prosperity, have forgotten to worship their Creator, call upon him earnestly in the day of trouble, when they feel that His power only can deliver them; but with Washington it was a custom, as one of his nephews thus relates: " One morning, at daybreak, an officer came to the general's quarters with despatches. As such communications usually passed through my hands, I took the papers from the messenger and directed my steps towards the general's room. Walking along the passage which led to his door, I heard a voice within. I paused, and distinctly recognised the voice of the general. Listening for a moment, when all was silent around, I found that he was earnestly engaged in prayer. *I knew this to be his habit,* and therefore retired, with the papers in my hand, till such time as I supposed he had finished the exercise, when I returned, knocked at his door, and was admitted." Thus, in obedience to Him whom he called " the Divine Author of our blessed religion," Washington, in the retirement of his chamber, prayed to his " Father who seeth in secret ;" and truly his " Father who seeth in secret" did " reward him openly."

The aspect of affairs now became more cheering. Silas Deane arrived from France with a treaty between the United States and the French government, which revived everywhere the drooping spirits of the people. General Howe about the same time sailed for England. He was an experienced officer in European tactics, but wanted energy, enterprise, and activity and was utterly unable to cope with Washington. He was succeeded by Sir Henry Clinton, also an officer of experience and reputation. The alliance with France, and its anticipated consequences, rendered an entire change of measures necessary on the part of the enemy, and the new commander prepared to evacuate Philadelphia, to concentrate his force at New York. This design was executed, and he marched through New Jersey with Washington hanging on his rear, eager to strike a blow. He had so long been harassed by the necessity of constantly retreating, that the idea of pursuit animated him to new exertions and new vigour. At last he had turned on his pursuers, and almost for the first time since he assumed the command, could he indulge the bias of his temper, which was ever in favour of decisive action.

Though still inferior in force, he was equal in numbers, and hoped that Sir Henry Clinton would afford him an opportunity of attack, in his march through New Jersey. He proposed the question to a council of officers, where it was opposed by Steuben, Du Portail, and General Lee. But this did not deter him, and he resolved that the enemy should not escape without a blow, if an opportunity for striking it occurred. The march of the British general was directed towards Middletown, whence he intended to embark for New York, and he had now arrived at Monmouth, a small town on high ground, not far from the bay of Amboy, and presenting a strong position. Another day's march would bring him to the heights of Middletown, where he would be unassailable. This was the last opportunity that might present itself, and Washington determined to avail himself of it. Accordingly he made dispositions for an attack the moment Sir Henry Clinton moved from the high ground at Monmouth, and General Lee was directed to assault his rear, while the remainder of the Americans opposed him on his flanks.

Early in the morning, the British army had taken up its line of march towards Middletown. Washington, hearing a firing, presumed that Lee was engaged, and came rapidly on to second him, when, to his astonishment, he found that officer in full retreat.

"In the name of God, General Lee, what has caused this ill-timed prudence?" said Washington.

"I know no man blessed with a larger portion of that rascally virtue than your excellency," retorted Lee, sarcastically.

Washington rode on furiously: for once in his life, ill-conduct, aggravated by insolence, had conquered his equanimity. He called to his men, and they answered him with cheers. He ordered them to charge, and they obeyed with enthusiasm. The English attempted to turn his flank, but were repulsed. They turned in another direction, and met Greene, who drove them back with his cannon, while Wayne, at the head of his legion, gave them such a severe fire, that they ceased to act on the offensive, and again took post in their stronghold. The extreme heat of the day, together with their exertions in the fight, had exhausted the vigour of both parties; some died of mere fatigue, and others fell victims to their eagerness to allay their burning thirst. Washington ordered his soldiers to prepare for renewing the action early in the morning; but when that came, the British had decamped, and were so far on their way to Middletown Heights as to destroy all hopes of preventing their embarkation.

On no occasion during the whole course of the war, did Washington appear greater than at Monmouth. He exposed himself to every danger, and seemed determined to make up by his own exertions for the misconduct of Lee, who was tried shortly after for disobedience of orders, for misbehaviour before the enemy, and for disrespect to the commander-in-chief. The sentence of the court suspended him from duty for one year, and was unanimously approved by Congress. This terminated his military career. He lived a few years an eccentric life, and finally died in deserved obscurity.

Washington received a letter from Congress, informing him that a French fleet had arrived off the coast of Virginia, and requesting him immediately to form some plan, in the execution of which the fleet could assist him. The admiral proposed attacking the English at Newport, in Rhode Island. Washington consented, and made preparations for doing so. American troops, commanded by General Sullivan, were soon in readiness to besiege the town, but waited some days for the French to appear and assist them. Confident that they were near, Sullivan commenced the siege. The fleet in a few days was in sight, but then moved off to meet the English naval force which had sailed from New York. They were prepared for an action, when a violent storm separated them, and injured several of their ships. The English sailed back to New York, and the French admiral informed General Sullivan, that he could not return to Newport, but would sail to Boston to repair his damages.

Sullivan was disappointed by this resolution, as it would oblige him to give up the siege, in which he had every prospect of success, if assisted by the

French. General Lafayette went to the admiral **to** prevail on him to remain, but his efforts were fruitless. Sullivan, in giving his orders to his troops, said they must " endeavour to do for themselves, what their friends had refused to aid them in ;" but he found it would be useless to continue the siege, and withdrew. He was followed by the English, and had a short but severe battle on the 29th August, when he crossed over to the main land. The next day a large land force and several English ships arrived at Newport, so that if he had remained one day longer, his army must have been destroyed or taken. The French admiral was very much offended by General Sullivan's remarks ; and the people in Boston were so much displeased with the conduct of the admiral, that it was feared he would not be able to get assistance there to repair his ships.

Washington watched every occurrence that would be likely to injure the interests of the country ; and this event gave him great uneasiness. He endeavoured to calm the offended parties ; and in this work he was aided by Lafayette, who was as dear to his own countrymen as to the Americans. A few letters passed between Washington and the admiral, and a good understanding was restored. When the English fleet was repaired, it sailed to Boston, to blockade the French; but a storm again drove it out to sea, and in the beginning of November the French sailed for the West Indies.

The danger of a war in Europe, in which the French would be interested, caused Lafayette to obtain leave of absence, and to return to his native country. A part of the English army was sent to the southern states; and as there was no prospect of doing any thing in the north in a winter campaign, Washington placed his army in quarters, the main body in Connecticut, and portions on both sides of the Hudson river, about West Point, and at Middle Brook.

CHAPTER VII.

T may be doubted whether the success of the American cause was greatly accelerated by the assistance afforded by France. The people, who before had relied solely upon their own energies, began now to think their triumph was secured, and from that moment to remit in some degree the exertions they would otherwise have made. Washington's efforts were unceasing, both with the army and the Congress, in warning against the dangers of a false security, and though in the next two years there were few military movements of much consequence, it may be doubted whether the Father of his Country ever served her interests more effectually than in this period. Still, the army was suffered to dwindle away until it amounted to less than three thousand; disaffection spread among the troops; the Connecticut line mutinied; and the farmers, having lost all faith in the ability of Congress to pav

for their produce, refused to trust any longer in the
promises of that body.

Among the military operations of the year, were
the melancholy destruction of Wyoming, in Pennsylvania, and the storming of Stoney Point. The
last act was gallantly accomplished by General
Wayne. Washington had in view an attack on the
enemy's posts at and about King's Ferry, which he
decided to take in detail, rather than risk a general
system of operations, which the failure of a single
link might render ineffectual. Stoney Point was one
of the most inaccessible of these, and in addition to
its natural strength, was defended by six hundred of
the enemy, under Colonel Johnson. It was intended
to take it by surprise, and for that purpose midnight
was chosen for the attack. The hour came, and
Wayne's little band marched in silence to execute
their purpose. There was but one way of approaching this strong position, and that was over a narrow
causeway, crossing a marsh. They advanced without speaking a word, with unloaded muskets and
fixed bayonets, preceded by the forlorn hope, consisting of two parties of twenty men each. They
gained the works without being discovered; for the
enemy little dreamed of an attempt on their strong
position. A few minutes after twelve, the attack

commenced ; the Americans dashed forward under
a heavy fire, and carried the fort at the point of the
bayonet, with the loss of about one hundred, killed
and wounded. The loss of the enemy was sixty
three killed, and upwards of five hundred prisoners.
Wayne received a slight wound in the head, which
stunned him for a few minutes; but, supported by
his aids, on either side, he continued at his post, and
entered the fort with the foremost of his associates.

This affair recalled the attention of Sir Henry
Clinton from Connecticut, whither he had sent an
expedition under Governor Tryon, and he advanced
up the Hudson, towards the Highlands, and re-
possessed himself of Stoney Point. Finding, how
ever, that he could not attack Washington with any
chance of success, in the strong position he occupied, the British commander fell back upon the
city, and devoted his attention to the affairs of the
south, whither the tide of war was now flowing.
Leaving a sufficient force to protect New York, he
carried the war into the south with more vigour
than ever. He besieged and took Charleston, which
surrendered the 12th of May, 1780, and with it
the whole southern army, under General Lincoln.

By this disaster the whole southern section of the

country was left exposed to the enemy. No assist-ance could be obtained from the American army in the north, which was now weakened in numbers, and by want and misery; so that General Schuyler wrote as follows to Washington on the subject:— "At one time the soldiers ate every kind of horse-feed but hay. As an army, they bore it with the most heroic patience; but sufferings like these, accompanied by the want of clothes, blankets, &c., will produce fre-quent desertion in all armies; and so it happened with us, though it did not create a single mutiny."

Another gloomy period succeeded the hopes awak-ened by the alliance with France. As yet it had done nothing but draw on the Americans a greater weight of vengeance. The French fleets were followed by superior fleets of the enemy, which checked their operations on our coasts; and when they departed for one place, took advantage of their absence to scourge those whom they came to protect. Con-gress could procure no supplies for the army in ex-change for promises, whose fulfilment depended on a distant hope. It became impossible to graduate the pay of the army to the rapid depression of the medium of payment. The pay of a field officer would not furnish provender for his horse, and that of a common soldier could find nothing necessary to

his comfort within the compass of his means. Owing
to a want of uniformity in the military establishment,
arising in a great degree from the different quotas
of the states being placed under the supervision of
those who sent them, and not of Congress directly,
and the means or will of some of the states being
greater than of others, it frequently happened that the
troops of one state would be, at least partially, supplied with necessaries or comforts, of which the
rest were wholly destitute. Thus, to the miseries
of want, was added the aggravation of seeing others
in comparative plenty; for though the soldiers
sometimes shared with each other, it was not to be
expected that they would strip themselves to clothe
a stranger, or divide their last morsel with any but
their dearest associates.

In this condition of things, a strong disposition to
mutiny began to manifest itself among the common
soldiers, which was not checked by an exertion of
the influence of the officers. They too were suffering like their fellows; those who had private fortunes were compelled to expend them, and those
who depended on their pay were left destitute by the
worthlessness of paper-money. The officers of more
than one line unanimously announced their determination to resign, and without doubt, if they had

AT THE SIEGE OF CHARLESTON.   Page 100.

carried this resolution into effect, it would have been followed by a voluntary disbandment of the whole, or a greater portion, of the army. But whenever the Genius of Freedom despaired, she had recourse .o the wisdom and influence of Washington. He called to him the officers who were about to take this fatal step; he reasoned with them on the duties of patriotism, and the sacrifices which every man owed to his country in the hour of peril; he referred to the past, as furnishing rational grounds of hope for the future, and by the force of his eloquence, aided by the weight of his character, at length induced them to devote themselves again to the cause in which they had suffered so much and so long. The immediate wants of the army were finally relieved by the expedient of a bank in Philadelphia, the object of which was the supply of provisions and clothing, by means of a capital of three hundred thousand pounds.

The enemy, who on all occasions miscalculated the patriotism of the people, presuming on the discontents of the army, in the beginning of June made an attempt in New Jersey. Five thousand men, under General Knyphausen, landed at Elizabethtown-point, and marched into the interior as far as Springfield. But the militia flew to arms, and gave them such a reception that they halted at Connecticut

Farms, after having in revenge set fire to that set
tlement.

In this period, Washington occupied the hills between Springfield and Chatham. His force consisted
of less than four thousand. Yet he never despaired
or remitted his exertions. He watched with inces-
sant vigilance for an opportunity of checking and
punishing the invader; he toiled himself; himself
set the example of fortitude and patience, while, at the
same time, what Providence had denied him to do by
his sword, he endeavoured to do with his pen. He
called upon those who directed the civil affairs of the
states to exert their influence and their energies to
enable him to defend the liberties of the country,
and never ceased urging them, with a dignified and
decorous firmness, to the adoption of measures for
the safety of the good cause. In many instances,
they were animated to the passage of laws for this
purpose; but the delays, perhaps difficulties, of carry
ing them into execution, were such as, in very many
cases, prevented Washington from availing himself
of their benefits until the opportunity had passed
away, never to return. There can be no doubt what
ever, that if his means had in any degree corresponded with those of the enemy, he would have finished the war in a single campaign. But this was

at no time the case, and least of all now. General
Knyphausen, finding it impossible to bring him to
action, or to take advantage of his rashness in the
admirable position he had chosen, returned once
more to Elizabethtown, there to wait the arrival of
Sir Henry Clinton from the south, which event took
place about the middle of June, and added to the
already overwhelming force of the enemy, who resumed his operations in New Jersey with new vigour.
But meeting with a brave resistance at the bridge
of Rahway, and discouraged by the spirit and vigour
displayed on that occasion by the regular troops
under General Greene, the British commander turned
back once more to Elizabethtown, whence he passed
over to Staten Island.

In the month of July following, the French fleet,
commanded by the Chevalier Ternay, having on
board six thousand troops, under Count Rochambeau,
appeared off Rhode Island. The anxiety of Washington had been extreme that the states should be prepared to co-operate with their allies with an efficient
force. The plan which he had urged for recruiting the
army had been partly adopted; but such were the
delays attending the action of government, and such
the discouragements which stood in the way of en-
listment, that he could form no reasonable esti

mate of the force with which he might be able to co-operate with the French, and consequently propose no feasible plan of operations. This was the more mortifying to his feelings, as the French army had been placed by the court of France entirely under his direction. The arrival rendered it now imperative on him to present to their commanders a definitive plan for the campaign. He accordingly communicated to them an arrangement for besieging New York, in the forlorn hope that the means of fulfilling his part would in time be furnished by Congress and the states. " Pressed on all sides," he says, in a letter to the former, "by a choice of difficulties, in a moment which requires decision, I have adopted that line of conduct which comported with the dignity and faith of Congress, the reputation of these states, and the honour of our arms. I have sent on definitive proposals of co-operation to the French general and admiral. Neither the period, the season, nor a regard to decency would permit delay. The die is cast; and it remains with the states, either to fulfil their engagements, preserve their credit, and support their independence, or to involve us in disgrace and defeat. Notwithstanding the failures pointed out by the committee, I shal proceed on the supposition that they will ultimately consult their own interest and honour, and not suffer us to fail for want of means which it is evidently in their power to afford. What has been done, and is doing, by some of the states, confirms the opinion I have entertained of sufficient resources in the country. Of the disposition of the people to submit to any arrangement for calling them forth, I see no reasonable ground of doubt. If we fail for want of proper exertions in any of the governments, I trust the responsibility will fall where it ought, and that I shall stand justified to Congress, my country, and the world."

The plan proposed for the siege of New York contemplated that the troops should leave Newport, and the Americans rendezvous at Morrisania, opposite the north end of York Island, where they were to form a junction. It was indispensable to the success of the arrangement that the French should possess a naval superiority over the British. But this was effectually prevented by the arrival of six ships of the line, sent by Admiral Graves to reinforce the squadron at New York. This turned the scales completely ; and instead of the allies besieging the British in New York, the English admiral sailed to Rhode Island to attack the French. At the same time Sir Henry Clinton proceeded with eight thousand men, with a design, as was supposed, of co-operation, and Washington prepared for an attack on New York in his absence. This brought Clinton back to his old quarters, which movement of course arrested the design of the American commander.

Thus all prospects of a junction of the a'lied forces of America and France were destroyed. The policy of the French in co-operating with the Americans had a twofold object: One was to assist America, the other to protect the French West India Islands. Hence, in the history of those times, the conduct of the French admirals, in appearing at one moment here, and the next sailing for the West Indies, is explained by the necessity of following the movements of the fleet of the enemy.

By the unexpected return of the Admiral Count de Guichen to France, which created great disappointment among both French and Americans, the British land and naval forces were each left in the ascendency, and the allies forced to act on the defensive. Washington, however, still cherished a determination to attempt New York the first opportunity; when the arrival of Admiral Rodney, with eleven ships of the line, rendered all further prosecution of the design hopeless, until a change should take place in the relative force of the parties.

CHAPTER VIII.

HEN the English had abandoned Philadelphia, General Benedict Arnold, who had been wounded in the north, and was still unfitted for the active services of the field, was placed in command of that city. He had often shown himself possessed of courage, and of military ability; and his patriotism had not yet, perhaps, been doubted. But the life of pleasure which opened before him, as he recovered from his wounds, presented too many temptations to vice, for his resistance; and he abandoned himself to dissipation and extravagance. The unbecoming means to which he resorted to obtain money, brought him into collision with the local authorities, and under the censure of Congress. He demanded a trial, and was sentenced to be reprimanded by Washington. His pride was deeply wounded, and the mild lesson he received from his

commander, instead of inducing his reform, determined him to deeper transgressions. Either before,
or soon afterwards, he entered into a correspondence
with the British in New York, and only waited to
become worth buying, to propose the purchase to
Sir Henry Clinton. That opportunity offered itself
when, at his solicitation, he was placed in command
of the post of West Point, which was the key to the
Highlands, the head-quarters of the American army,
and the very stronghold of our cause. He now
meditated the final consummation of his treason.
In conjunction with Major John Andre, adjutant-
general of the British army, he matured a plan,
which, had it been successfully executed, would in
all probability have resulted in the capture of the
entire army, and all the military stores deposited at
West Point. Sir Henry Clinton was to proceed by
water to the Highlands with all his force, where he
would find the American troops dispersed in situations which would render defence impossible and
their capture certain. The absence of Washington
in Connecticut furnished the favourable moment.
To give the last finish to this fatal scheme, the Vulture sloop of war was sent up the river, as near the
Highlands as was prudent, bearing Andre to an in-
terview with Arnold who had come down to Haver-

straw for this purpose. Accordingly they met, and settled the final preliminaries of this momentous project. But Providence, who seems ever to have watched over the liberties of the United States, interposed a series of obstacles, apparently trifling in themselves, but decisive in their consequences. Andre was to have been put on board the Vulture by daylight in the morning, but that vessel had been obliged to remove so far down the river, by a fire from the shore, from a small cannon, that the men appointed to row the boat, which belonged to a man of the name of Smith, refused to perform the task. They either feared detection, suspected something wrong, or were, as they pleaded, too much fatigued for such a service.

It then became necessary to provide for the return of Andre by land. The country between the Highlands and Kingsbridge was at that period called "between the lines," and was subject to the inroads of both parties.

As it was possible Andre might encounter some of the Americans on his route, it was determined, after much alleged opposition on his part, that he should ay aside his uniform and put on a disguise. Thus relinquishing his character of soldier, he was passed over to the east side of the river, and fur-

nished by Smith with a horse. Smith also accompanied him as far as he thought necessary or prudent, and then, bidding him farewell, returned to his
home. Andre pursued his way without meeting any
interruption, or encountering a single obstacle, and
was congratulating himself, as he afterwards declared, on being now in safety, when, in the act of
crossing a little bridge, near the village of Tarry-
town, he was stopped by a young man, who darted
out of the woods and seized his bridle. Completely
taken by surprise, he acted as men usually do in
such situations. He asked the young man, whose
name was John Paulding, where he came from? He
replied, " From below," a phrase signifying that he
came from the British posts in that direction. "And
so do I," cried Andre, expecting to be immediately
released. But this confession betrayed him, and on
the appearance of two other young men, named
Williams and Van Wart, who were called out by
the first, he discovered his imprudence. It was then
that he produced his pass from Arnold, which would
probably have assured his release, but for the previous declaration, that he came " from below." He
was taken into an adjoining wood, and searched,
without making the least resistance; and nothing
being found to excite suspicion, the young men began

to waver under his threats of the vengeance of Arnold, should they detain him.

Before they let him go, however, it was proposed to search his boots, which had hitherto escaped their attention; and now, for the first time, Andre turned pale. He discovered an unwillingness that excited suspicion, and they were obliged to resort to threats before they could induce him to submit. On pulling off his right boot, a paper was discovered, which at once indicated his business. It was a plan of West Point, the disposition of the army, and of every particular necessary to the success of the British. This, and other papers, all in the handwriting of Arnold, disclosed the importance of the prize.

There are not in history many nobler examples of patriotism than that of these young Americans. They were the sons of reputable families in the county of Westchester, but they were poor, and their poverty had been rendered more pressing by the evils and excesses of war. Their parents lived " between the lines," and were equally subjected to the injuries of both parties. Andre offered them any reward they should demand, and pledged himself to remain as a hostage wherever they pleased until the reward was received. " If you would give me ten thousand guineas, you should go nowhere but to head-quar ters," replied Paulding, and the sentiment was echoeu by Williams and Van Wart.

As they proceeded to the quarters of the nearest officer, Andre remained at first silent and sad, unti they stopped for refreshment at a small country inn. Here he entered into some conversation with the young men, and seemed more cheerful. During the rest of their journey he scarcely uttered a word.

The capture of Andre disconcerted for ever the nefarious schemes of Arnold. Jameson, the officer to whom he was conducted, who seems to have been a weak and credulous man, permitted Andre to write the traitor a letter announcing his capture, in the expectation, probably, that he would take measures for nis release. But the only use he made of the information was to flee with all speed, leaving his wife to the mercy of those he attempted to betray, and his name to their execrations. He succeeded in reaching the Vulture, whence he proceeded to New York. Here he met the rewards of that treason which the virtue of three poor youths had defeated; he received from the British general the rank he had forfeited in the American army; distinguished himself by his impertinence, his gasconade, and his cruelties; retired to England at the conclusion of the war, where he lived

a life of mortification, poverty, and worthlessness, and died a death worthy of his never-ending infamy.

Andre, perceiving the impossibility of further deception, wrote to Washington, announcing his name and rank, and hinting that the treatment of certain prisoners taken at Charleston might materially depend on that which he received. His subsequent conduct was manly and becoming; he was tried, condemned, and executed as a spy, amid the regrets of his enemies, who, in consideration of his youth, and the circumstances of his death, lamented his fate, and wished for some other victim.

He had, however, no cause of complaint, and according to the usages of war, with which he was familiar, he merited his fate. While a prisoner he was treated with kindness and courtesy. His life would have been spared if the public welfare had permitted. Very different was the treatment of an American officer, Captain Hale, who was arrested by the English, under less aggravated circumstances, on Long Island. He was in all respects the equal of Andre, and superior to him in that he perilled life for his country's freedom, while Andre was a mere mercenary soldier. Hale was subjected to the most unfeeling brutality by the English officers; denied the privilege of writing to his family; denied the

H

consolations of religion; denied every thing which in civilized communities it is the custom to yield to even the vilest criminals. Hale is forgotten by his countrymen, while Andre, an enemy who sought our ruin, and who, perhaps, would have caused us the lives of thousands, had not the patriotism of Paulding and his companions been proof against his gold, is a favourite hero of our romancers and poets.

There were but few military operations under the immediate command of Washington during the campaign of 1780, and those which occurred were of slight importance. General Greene, who had been appointed to the command of the army in the south, prosecuted the war in that quarter with vigour and with some success. The battle of the Cowpens, which was fought on the 17th of January, 1781, between the American forces under General Morgan, and the English under Colonel Tarleton, was the most decisive triumph of our arms in that winter; the loss of the Americans being but eighty in killed and wounded, while Cornwallis lost about one-fifth of his army, besides arms, ammunition, and other military stores. Morgan was, however, soon compelled to retreat into Virginia, before the main body of the British, who endeavoured to retrieve the loss sustained by Tarleton at the Cowpens.

On the first of January, thirteen hundred men, stationed at Morristown, New Jersey, threatened to lay down their arms and return home, unless Congress granted them redress of grievances. No doubt they acted wrongly; but, however reprehensible their conduct may seem, it originated in no unworthy motives. It was the consequence of personal hardship and suffering, not of disaffection or cowardice. When Wayne, their commander, threatened them with a cocked pistol, they exclaimed, with one voice, "General, we love you, we respect you, but if you fire you are a dead man. We are not going to desert to the enemy. Were he in sight at this moment, you would see us fight under your orders in defence of our country. We love liberty, but we cannot starve." Their subsequent conduct proved the truth of their professions. When Sir Henry Clinton, hearing of these proceedings, despatched emissaries to tempt them to his side, by a promise of reward, they spurned his proposals, seized his emissaries, and delivered them up to their general. Such behaviour, in some measure, atoned for their mutiny. Washington was at New Windsor, on the Hudson, when news of the revolt reached him, which was before the civil authorities of Pennsylvania had yielded in a great measure to the claims which they presented

He felt the justice of the demands of the poor sol·
diers, and the danger of compliance. To deny them
might be followed by perseverance in the course
they had taken ; to yield to threats, made with arms
in their hands, would, beyond doubt, encourage
others having equal cause of complaint, to pursue a
similar cause. He, therefore, declined to interpose
his personal authority.

No immediate danger could result from the withdrawal of the Pennsylvania line in the dead of winter,
and now was, perhaps, the best time to impress upon
Congress and the state authorities the necessity of
providing for the future pay and wants of the army.
Accordingly, he contented himself with recommending to General Wayne a watchful vigilance over the
movements of other portions of the army in his vicinity, and advising him to draw the refractory line
to the western side of the Delaware, for the purpose
of rendering it more difficult for the enemy to tam-
per with them in their present state of excitement.
The authorities of Pennsylvania having yielded to
the claims of these soldiers, the consequences of
their success were soon visible in other divisions of
the army. A considerable portion of the Jersey
brigade made demands similar to those so successfully asserted by the Pennsylvania line, and there

was reason to fear that a general disaffection would ere long manifest itself by similar effects in other divisions. Washington had foreseen the consequences of complying with demands which, though not unjust, were ill-timed, and made in a manner destructive to military discipline. Perceiving that every additional example of successful mutiny would be a signal for others, he determined to take decisive measures towards the Jersey brigade. He directed General Howe to march against the new mutineers; to quell the resistance at all hazards; to make no terms with them under any circumstances; and whether they surrendered their arms, or resisted by force, to seize and hang a few of the ringleaders in the presence of their confederates. No resistance was made; they laid down their arms, and two of the most active were shot. The remainder returned to their duty to a country, which nothing but a series of hardships and privations, difficult for the most patriotic to bear, had induced them, in a moment of impatient suffering, to desert.

Washington made use of this revolt to show to Congress, and to the different states, the necessity of making more effectual exertions to supply the army with clothing and food. He represented their sufferings so feelingly, that efforts were made in each state to contribute to their relief; and small as the aid was, the sufferers were satisfied with this proof that their countrymen were not unmindful of them. When Congress had succeeded in satisfying the discontented troops, they entered upon the dis· cussion of a plan for a union of the states which would enable them to carry on the war with less difficulty and expense. Articles of confederation were drawn up, and agreed to by all the members of Congress, and the knowledge of this bond of union gave universal satisfaction.

All the accounts which Washington heard from the southern states made him anxious to send more troops there. The French fleet had been blockaded at Newport by the English; but a violent storm injured many of the English ships, and on being moved away, the French admiral was enabled to send out a portion of his force, which he directed to sail to the Chesapeake. When Washington heard of this, he resolved to send troops to Virginia, in the expectation that he could obtain aid from the French in attacking some of the ports which were in possession of the enemy. The French ships, however, soon returned to Newport. Washington was thus disappointed in his hope of aid at that time, but he sent troops, under Lafayette, to Virginia; and went to

Newport to communicate to the French admiral a plan which he had formed for co-operation. The admiral agreed to his proposals, and sent out a part of his vessels, but they were met by the English, and, after a sharp action, separated, and returned again to Newport.

A portion of the troops which were marching to the south under Lafayette, became discontented, and he discovered that desertions were constantly occurring. He called together all who remained, and told them he would not deceive them as to the difficulties and dangers to which they would be exposed, but, that any individual who was unwilling to encounter them, should have permission to return to the army in New Jersey. This generosity had the desired effect.

A large force had been sent from New York to Arnold, and Cornwallis had joined him, and taken command of all the troops. With so large an army he was certain to defeat the little band of Lafayette, which he heard had entered Virginia, and he determined to attack it as soon as possible. Lafayette wished to avoid Cornwallis, until the arrival of some reinforcements, which were on their way to join him, under General Wayne. Cornwallis heard of this, and determined to prevent it. He was so confident of success, that he wrote, in a letter which was intercepted, " the boy cannot escape me." But Lafayette moved with so much judgment and quickness, that his confident enemy was soon convinced he could not overtake him, or prevent his being joined by the expected troops, and he gave up the pursuit to wait for his return.

When Lafayette received the expected reinforcements, he turned, and was soon within a few miles of Cornwallis, who, suspecting that he intended securing some military stores that had been sent up the James river to Albemarle Court House, placed troops in a situation to attack him on the road which he supposed he would take. Lafayette anticipated this, and in the night opened an old road, which had been long unused, by which he marched quietly to his destination; and in the morning, when Cornwallis had expected to have him in his power, he had the mortification of discovering that he had passed by, and was in a situation in which he could not be attacked. He probably thought the American army was larger than it really was; for he gave up the intention he had formed of forcing it to an action, and marched to Williamsburg. Lafayette followed him with great caution, and attacked several companies that were moving about the country, but avoided the danger of an engagement with the main army.

While the British fleet was lying in the Potomac, in the vicinity of Mount Vernon, a message was sent to the overseer, demanding a supply of fresh provisions. The usual penalty of a refusal was setting fire to the house and barns of the owner. To prevent this destruction of property, the overseer, on receipt of the message, gathered a supply of provisions, and went himself on board with a flag, accompanying the present with a request that the property of the general might be spared. Washington was indignant at this proceeding. "It would," he writes, "have been a less painful circumstance to me to have heard that, in consequence of your noncompliance with the request of the British, they had burned my house, and laid my plantation in ruins. You ought to have considered yourself as my representative, and should have reflected on the bad example of communicating with the enemy, and making a voluntary offer of refreshment to them with a view to prevent a conflagration."

CHAPTER IX.

ALL Washington's plans for the reduction of New York were destined from various causes to fail. He had looked forward to the fall of that city as the last important act of the war, and had more than once completed as nearly as was possible his arrangements for an attack upon it; but the happy combination of resources and opportunity had not been presented, and he somewhat reluctantly now turned his attention toward the South. The appearance of a design to lay siege to New York was, however, kept up, with a view of deceiving Sir Henry Clinton, and preventing his sending assistance to Cornwallis, who had strongly urged and received his promise of large reinforcements. The design was rendered successful by a perseverance in all the common preparations for a siege, and particularly by the interception of a letter written by Washington at the time when it was really his intention to attack New York, detailing the plan of his intended operations. Nothing could be more fortunate than the destination of this letter. It confirmed Clinton so strongly in the impression that a siege was determined upon, even after it was abandoned, that nothing could shake his conviction. He was strengthening his defences and husbanding his force, until the American army was far on its way to Virginia. He then prepared to reinforce Cornwallis, but he was five days too late.

Washington left the neighbourhood of New York towards the end of August, after having so fully impressed the British commander with the idea that his intention was to lay siege to the city, that he considered this movement a mere feint to deceive him. It was not until too late to overtake the combined armies, that he became certain of their real destination.

Sensible that the success of the design against Cornwallis depended altogether on anticipating the reinforcements which it was presumed Sir Henry Clinton would send him, as soon as his apprehensions for the safety of New York were removed, Washington proceeded towards the head of Chesapeake Bay. He marched rapidly through New Jersey and Pennsylvania; received at Chester the news of the arrival of the French fleet under Count de Grasse, and embarking the principal part of his army at the head of the Elk, proceeded to Williamsburg, where he met the French admiral, with whom the plan of operations was settled.

The departure from New York was the signal for an invasion of Connecticut by the enemy. Arnold, who had ravaged Virginia, now volunteered to invade his native state. The storming of Fort Griswold, the death of Colonel Ledyard, the massacre of the garrison, and the burning of New London, constitute the closing chapter of the traitor's life of shame and guilt, and give the finish to his career.

The moment was now approaching which had been looked for, sometimes in hope, but oftener in despair. The great question was now to be decided. Cornwallis, at the head of upwards of seven thousand men, with a great train of artillery, had taken a position at York, a small town at the northern verge of the peninsula, between York and James Rivers, about eight miles wide. The town occupies the summit of a high abrupt bank, on the south side of the river. He has been blamed for cooping his army up in a place whence there was no retreat in case of defeat; but he calculated on the superiority

BENEDICT ARNOLD AT THE BURNING OF NEW LONDON.   Page 124.

of the British naval force, which would at all times afford him the means of escape, and the facility in receiving reinforcements from Sir Henry Clinton.

The arrival of Count de Grasse with twenty-five ships of the line destroyed one ground of hope, and the delays of Clinton were equally fatal to the other. He saw himself besieged by a superior army, animated by the certainty of success; every day increased his difficulties, and diminished his hopes of assistance; new batteries were raised on all sides against him, while his own defences fell, one after another; the Americans and French vied in acts of gallantry, and at the expiration of a few days his situation became desperate. Cornwallis wrote to Washington to request that hostilities might cease for twenty-four hours, during which time he would inform him on what terms he would surrender. Washington informed him that it was his ardent desire to spare the shedding of blood, and that he would listen with readiness to such terms as could be accepted; but requested that they might be made known immediately in writing, as he could quickly determine if he would agree to them.

To some of the proposals of Cornwallis, Washington could not consent, and he wrote the terms on which he expected him to lay down his arms, and said he would not change them. They were, that all the army, with their arms and military stores, and all the ships and seamen, were to be delivered up, the troops to be prisoners to Congress, and the naval force to the French. The soldiers were to remain, with a few officers, in America; and the rest of the officers to return to Europe on assurance that they would not serve again against America. Cornwallis was to be allowed to send a ship unsearched to New York, to carry any papers he chose to send there. These terms were accepted by the English general, and on the 19th of October, 1781, the whole British army marched out of York-town, as prisoners of war. General Lincoln was appointed by Washington to receive the submission of the enemy, in the same manner in which Cornwallis had received that of the Americans on the 12th of May, 1780, at Charleston.

While the troops of Cornwallis were marching out of the town, with cased colours and drums beating the sad sound of defeat, Washington said to his men, " My brave fellows, let no sensation of satisfaction for the triumph you have gained, induce you to insult a fallen enemy; let no shouting, no clamorous huzzaing, increase their mortification It is a sufficient satisfaction to us that we witness their humiliation. Posterity will huzza for us!"

On the day after the surrender, he ordered that all who were under arrest should be set at liberty, and he closed his order with this direction, " Divine service shall be performed to-morrow in the different divisions of the army; and the commander-in-chief recommends that all the troops that are not upon duty do assist at it, with a serious deportment, and that sensibility of heart, which the recollection of the surprising and particular interposition of Divine Providence in our favour, claims."

The force surrendered amounted to more than seven thousand men, with a train of upwards of one hundred and sixty pieces of cannon. The scene had scarcely closed when Clinton appeared at the mouth of the Chesapeake with a reinforcement equal to the number who had just laid down their arms. But he came too late. The news was communicated to him, that all was over with Cornwallis, and he returned to New York.

The capture of the Southern army awakened a thrill from one end of the United States to the other It was everywhere hailed as the finishing of the war, the end of a long series of hardships and sufferings. There was scarcely a city, town, or village, throughout the whole Confederation that had not felt the scourge; few were the fields that escaped ravaging, or the houses that had not been plundered, and few the citizens but had suffered in their persons or property. The whirlwind had not confined itself to one narrow track; it had swept over the face of the country from north to south, from east to west; it had crossed and recrossed its path in every direction, and wherever it had passed had left its mark of ruin.

The prospect of winning the prize for which all these sufferings had been patiently endured, awakened the gladness of the whole people. In the dead of the night, a watchman in the streets of Philadelphia was heard to cry out, "Past twelve o'clock, and a pleasant morning — Cornwallis is taken." The city became alive; the candles were lighted, and figures might be seen flitting past the windows, or pushing them up, to hear the sound repeated, lest it should have been nothing but a dream. The citizens ran through the streets to inquire into the truth. None slept again that night, and the dawn, which brought confirmation of the happy tidings, shone on one of the most exulting cities that ever basked in the sunshine of triumph.

WASHINGTON AT THE SIEGE OF YORKTOWN.   Page 126.

CHAPTER X.

THROUGHOUT the country, ar.d throughout the world, which had been a deeply interested spectator of the conflict, the capture of this second British army was regarded as decisive of our struggle for independence. The combined army soon after separated to go into winter quarters.

A portion of the French forces departed for the West Indies, and the residue remained in Virginia until the spring, when it left the country, followed by the blessings of the people.

Washington, after separating from the French, resumed his position on the Hudson, for the purpose of being ready to act, if necessary, against Sir Henry Clinton on the opening of the spring. Though hoping the war was now closed, he did not remit his exertions to be prepared for its renewal. He saw the necessity of being ready for another campaign

I

" I shall endeavour," he writes to General Greene, who so nobly distinguished himself in the war of the South—" I shall endeavour to stimulate Congress to .he best improvement of our success, by taking the most vigorous and effectual measures to be ready for an early and decisive campaign the next year. My greatest fear is, that, viewing this stroke in a point of light which may too much magnify its importance, they may think our work too nearly closed, and fall into a state of languor and relaxa- tion. To prevent this error, I shall employ every means in my power; and if unhappily we fall into this fatal mistake, no part of the blame shall be mine."

But, on receiving news of the capture of Corn- wallis, the ministry ceased to have a majority in the House of Commons in favour of the war. Various motions were made for putting an end to it, and finally a resolution was passed, declaring that the House would consider as enemies to the king and to the country all who should advise or attempt the further prosecution of offensive war in America. The command of the forces in this country was given to Sir Guy Carleton, with instructions to pre- pare the way for an accommodation by every proper means in his power.

Carleton accordingly opened a correspondence with Congress, proposing the appointment of commissioners on their part to negotiate a reconciliation. By the terms of the treaty of alliance between the United States and France, neither party could conclude a separate peace without the consent of the other, and the negotiations were transferred to Paris. Here, on the 30th of November, 1782, the provisional articles of a treaty were agreed on by John Adams, Benjamin Franklin, John Jay, and Henry Laurens, on the part of the United States, and Messrs. Fitzherbert and Oswald on behalf of Great Britain. The definitive treaty of peace was, however, not finally ratified until the 30th of September, 1783. It recognised the independence of the United States, and for ever.

Thus, after a series of sacrifices as great as was perhaps ever made by any nation for the attainment of freedom, and an accumulation of sufferings, hardships, disappointments, and aggravated difficulties, which could only have been borne by a brave, steady, and virtuous people, the United States won for themselves a station among the independent nations.

When the American army had the expectation of soon being dismissed from service, they became

anxious about the pay that was due them, and which
it was necessary they should receive, to enable them
to return to their families. An artful address was
circulated through the camp on the Hudson, for the
purpose of inducing desperate resolutions to force
the government to a compliance with their demands.
The address was accompanied by an invitation to
all the officers to meet on the next day, and take the
subject into consideration. Washington was in
camp, and his firmness and judgment did not forsake him. In his general orders he noticed the
address, and expressed his belief that the good sense
of the officers would prevent their " paying any attention to such an irregular invitation," but invited
them to meet on another day, when, he said, they
could deliberate on what course they ought to pursue. Before that day arrived, he conversed separately with the officers, and used his influence to
lead them to adopt measures which he intended to
propose. When they were assembled, he addressed
them in a calm and affectionate manner; entreating
them to disregard the efforts that were made to induce them to act disgracefully, and assuring them
of his confidence that Congress would treat them
justly.

This address, from one whom they loved and had

been accustomed to obey,—in whose judgment and affection they had perfect confidence,—could not fail to influence the army, and the officers immediately formed resolutions which satisfied their anxious commander, and proved their respect for him. It has been suggested that in no instance did the United States receive a more signal deliverance through the hands of Washington, than in the termination of this transaction. His conduct gave a new proof of the soundness of his judgment, and the purity of his patriotism. He wrote to Congress an account of what had occurred, and earnestly entreated that the demands of the army might be attended to, and that provision might be made for a further compensation than the mere pay which was due to the officers. He said, " if (as has been suggested for the purpose of inflaming their passions,) the officers of the army are to be the only sufferers by this revolution; if retiring from the field they are to grow old in poverty, wretchedness and contempt, and owe the miserable remnant of that life to charity, which has hitherto been spent in honour, then shall I have learned what ingratitude is ; then shall I have realized a tale which will embitter every moment of my future life."

Congress received a petition from the officers, and

then formed a resolution that, in addition o what was due to them, they should receive full pay for five years; but they knew some time would pass before the money could be raised. The officers were satisfied with the promise, and in the course of the summer a large portion of the troops returned to their homes.

A few new recruits, who had been stationed at Lancaster, marched to Philadelphia and placed sentinels at the doors of the State House, where Congress were sitting, and threatened to attack them if their demands for pay were not granted within twenty minutes. They did not perform their threat, but kept Congress prisoners for three hours. When Washington heard of this he sent fifteen hundred men to quell the mutineers, but this had been done without any violence before the troops arrived. He wrote to Congress that he felt much distressed on hearing of the insult which had been offered by these " soldiers of a day," and contrasted their conduct with that of the men who had " borne the heat and burden of the war; veterans, who have patiently endured nakedness, hunger and cold ; who have suffered and bled without a murmur, and who with perfect good order had retired to their homes without a settlement of their accounts, or a farthing of money in their pockets." In consequence of this event, Congress adjourned, to meet at Princeton, in New Jersey, at the close of the month of June, 1783. It sat there, in the Library room of the College, about three months, and then adjourned to meet at Annapolis, in Maryland.

When Washington had proclaimed the peace to his army on the 19th of April, he said, "On such a happy day—a day which completes the eight years of the war—it would be ingratitude not to rejoice, it would be insensibility not to participate in the general felicity;" and he directed that the chaplains, with their several brigades, should "render thanks to Almighty God for all his mercies, particularly for his overruling the wrath of man to his own glory; and causing the rage of war to cease among the nations." When he dismissed the troops from service on the 2d of November, he gave them serious and affectionate advice as to their future conduct: and assured them that he should recommend them to their grateful country, and in his prayers "to the God of armies." Earnestly desiring that his countrymen might secure a continuance of the favour of heaven, he wrote an address to the governors of the different states, which he said he wished them to consider as "the legacy of one who had ardently

desired on all occasions to be useful to his country;
and who, even in the shade of retirement, would not
fail to implore the divine benediction upon it." The
address contained important and wise counsel, and
he concluded it with the assurance, " I now make it
my earnest prayer that God would have you and
the state over which you preside in his holy protection, and that he would incline the hearts of the citizens to cultivate a spirit of subordination and obedience to government, and to entertain a brotherly
affection and love for one another ; for their fellow
citizens of the United States at large, and particularly for their brethren who have served in the field,
and, finally, that he would be most graciously pleased
to dispose us all to do justice, to love mercy, and to
demean ourselves with that charity, humility, and
pacific temper of mind, which were the characteristics of the Divine Author of our blessed religion ;
without an humble imitation of whose example in
these things we can never hope to be a happy na·
tion."

CHAPTER XI

HE final evacuation of New York by the British, occurred on the 25th of November, 1782. They had held possession of the city six years. Soon after their withdrawal, the American troops, under General Knox, took possession. They were followed by General Washington and Governor Clinton, who made a public entry on horseback, followed by civil and military officers, and a large number of citizens. Several days were devoted to festivities. The people of every class participated in the general joy.

Washington began now to prepare for revisiting his home at Mount Vernon, which he had not seen from the time on which he left it to take the command of the army. The most impressive and the most painful duty before him was to take leave of his old companions in arms. On the 4th of December, at twelve o'clock, they assembled, by his request, at the hotel in which he lodged, where in a few minutes they were met by their general. Few words passed, for their hearts were too full to speak Washington filled a glass of wine, turned to his fellow-soldiers, and, in a voice almost choked with his emotions, addressed them in these noble and affecting words: "With a heart full of love and gratitude, I now take leave of you. I most devoutly wish that your latter days may be as prosperous and happy as your former ones have been glorious and honourable." Having pledged himself to them all, he added,—"I cannot come to each of you to take my leave, but shall be obliged if each of you would come and take me by the hand." The first that came was General Knox, who received the pressure of his hand in silence, and in silence returned it. He was followed, one by one, by each of the officers present, who reciprocated the cordial embrace without uttering a word. A tear from the heart filled every eye; but no word could be uttered to break the silence of the affecting scene. Washington left the room, and the officers followed him, in noiseless procession, and with sad countenances, to the boat which was to convey him away from them. He stepped into it, and, turning towards the shore, waved his hat without speaking, the officers returned the salutation, and continued to gaze after their beloved commander until they could no longer distinguish his form, and then returned in sadness to the place where they had assembled.

Washington could not rest until he had performed all the duties which his upright mind dictated, and he proceeded to Philadelphia to give an account of the manner in which he had expended the public money. All his accounts were written by himself, and every entry made in the most exact manner, so as to give the least trouble in comparing them with the receipts with which they were accompanied. He made no charge for his services, but had spent a considerable portion of his own fortune. The regularity and minuteness with which he had kept an account of the funds received and expended during eight years, and the faithfulness with which he had, in the midst of his many employments, attended to having the public treasure used in the most economical and advantageous manner, proved that he had a right to the title of *an honest man.* From Philadelphia he proceeded to Annapolis, where Congress was sitting, and there he proved his patriot ism by giving back the power which had been placed in his hands, when he could no longer use it for the benefit of his country. Congress appointed the 23d

December for receiving his resignation, and a crowd of spectators witnessed the interesting ceremony. He was received by Congress as the " founder and guardian of the republic." Feeling the importance of the blessings of freedom and peace which the Great Ruler of the universe had made him an agent to obtain for them, they looked at him, when about to resign his power, with emotions of admiration and gratitude; and, recollecting how closely they had been connected with him in scenes of distress and danger, there were few eyes undimmed with tears. With unambitious dignity he rose and addressed General Mifflin, the President of Congress. He said, "I resign with satisfaction the appointment I accepted with diffidence; a diffidence in my abilities to accomplish so arduous a task, which, however, was superseded by a confidence in the rectitude of our cause, the support of the supreme power of the union, and the patronage of heaven. The successful termination of the war has verified the most sanguine expectations; and my gratitude for the interposition of Providence, and the assistance I have received from my countrymen, increase with every review of the momentous contest. I consider it as an indispensable duty to close this last act of my official life, by commending the interests of our dear-

WASHINGTON PARTING WITH HIS OLD COMRADES.   Page 138.

est country to the protection of Almighty God, and
those who have the superintendence of them to his
holy keeping. Having now finished the work as-
signed me, I retire from the great theatre of action,
and bidding an affectionate farewell to this august
body, under whose orders I have so long acted, I
here offer my commission, and take my leave of all
the employments of public life." He then gave his
commission to the President, who, when he had received it, answered him in the name of Congress,
and said, " Having defended the standard of liberty
in this new world: having taught a lesson useful to
those who inflict, and to those who feel oppression,
you retire from the great theatre of action with the
blessings of your fellow-citizens; but the glory of
your virtues will not terminate with your military
command; it will continue to animate remotest
ages. We join you in commending the interests
of our dearest country to the protection of Almighty
God, beseeching him to dispose the hearts and minds
of its citizens to improve the opportunity afforded
to them of becoming a happy and respectable nation. And for you, we address to Him our earnest
prayers, that a life so beloved may be fostered with
all his care that your days may be as happy as

they have been illustrious; and that he will finally give you that reward which this world cannot give."

History presents no more sublime scene than that of a successful hero, at the close of a long war, giving up his power, and a nation which has just achieved its independence, in the solemn act of dissolving its military state, all uniting in ascribing praise to God. "It seems impossible to contemplate the scene just sketched," remarks Mr. Paulding, "without feeling the heart to swell with the noblest, most affecting emotions. The event itself, so simple yet so grand; the example of a great and virtuous man, who, having fulfilled the duties for which he was raised to power, voluntarily comes forward to surrender it into the hands of the representatives of the people; the character and dignity of that august assembly to whom the trust was surrendered, and of the man who thus easily divested himself of authority; the piety, fervour, and simplicity of the address and the reply; and the recollection of the events which preceded and followed the consummation of the independence of a great nation—all combine to form a picture to which few of this world present a parallel. Here, as in all the acts of his life, Washington exhibited an example which will be much oftener admired than imitated

Here, as in all other circumstances, he stands almost alone in the world—great, without seeming to be great, because he performed great actions with such ease and simplicity, with such a total absence of all apparent effort, that, until we examine them critically, they appear like those of ordinary men."

When Washington had resigned the title of Commander-in-chief, he took that of private citizen, and retired to his peaceful home. The satisfaction he felt in doing so was expressed in a letter to his friend Lafayette, who had returned to France soon after the surrender of Cornwallis. " At length," he wrote, " I have become a private citizen, on the banks of the Potomac, and under the shade of my 'own vine and my own fig-tree,' and free from the bustle of a camp and the busy cares of public life I have not only retired from all public employments, but am retiring within myself, and shall be able to view the solitary walk, and tread the paths of private life, with heartfelt satisfaction." To General Knox he wrote,—"I feel now, as I conceive a weary traveller must do, who, after treading many a painful step, with a heavy burden on his shoulders, is eased of the latter, having reached the haven to which all the former were directed,—and from his house-top, in looking back and tracing with eager

eye, the meanders by 'which he has escaped the
quicksands and mires which lay in his way, and into
which none but the all-powerful Guide and Dispenser
of human events could have prevented his falling."
—For months after his return, he received, almost
every day, addresses from all parts of the union,
expressing the affection and gratitude of his countrymen.

He was at this time fifty-one years of age, with a
vigorous frame, and a constitution unbroken by the
vicissitudes of a hard service of eight arduous years,
notwithstanding in some of his letters he alludes to
his being occasionally afflicted with rheumatic pains,
the consequence of his former exposures in the field.
His pleasure was in the performance of his duties.
His employment was agriculture. He wished to set
an example of successful farming to all who were
within the sphere of his influence, and his long absence from the care of his estate left ample room
for improvements. Accordingly, he opened a correspondence with the most distinguished agricul-
turists of England and the United States, and availed
himself on all occasions of their experience, whenever he thought it applicable to the condition or the
means of his countrymen and neighbours.

Every morning he was abroad in the fields, direct-

ing his labourers, and seeing that they had complied
with his instructions. His eye was everywhere, and
as those who performed their duties never failed of
being rewarded by his approbation, so those who
neglected them were sure of a reprimand. He considered indulgence to his dependants, when carried
to the extent of permitting idleness or offence, as
equally unjust to himself and injurious to them. He
was a kind master to the good, a strict disciplinarian
to the bad, and he was both feared and loved by all
within the sphere of his domestic influence. He
exacted obedience, and repaid it by benefits. His
domestic government was patriarchal; the people
of his establishment were his children, equally the
subjects of his authority and the objects of his
affection.

But Washington did not confine himself to the
improvement of his own domain, or the introduction
of a better system of agriculture in his native state
He took journeys in different directions, to ascertain
the practicability of great internal improvements,
which might at one and the same time increase the
means of happiness, and, by associating the interests
of the different sections of the country, operate as
new bonds of union. His influence and his arguments prevailed in the legislature of Virginia, and

K

two companies were established for the purpose of extending the navigation of the Potomac and James Rivers. By the act of the legislature, one hundred and fifty shares of stock, amounting to forty thousand dollars, were offered to his acceptance. These he declined with a noble disinterestedness, and at his request they were appropriated to the purposes of education. Thus usefully and honourably employed in cultivating the earth, and forwarding objects beneficial to mankind, his short interval of repose passed away in all the comforts of a good man's lot. Health, competence, and well-won honour, active employment, and the recollections of a glorious life, all combined to make him as happy as is compatible with the dispensations of this world. —Washington on his farm at Mount Vernon, performing his duties as a virtuous and useful citizen, is not less worthy of contemplation than Washington leading his country to independence, and showing her how to enjoy it afterwards. The former example is indeed more extensively useful, because it comes home to the business and bosoms of ordinary men, and is within the reach of their imitation.

Among the pleasures which now awaited Washington was a visit from Lafayette, who, after the fall of Cornwallis, had gone back to France. It was, however, of short duration, for the friends were soon again engaged in public scenes and cares. Before Lafayette returned, he visited the mother of Washington. She received him kindly, and talked with him of the happy prospects of her country, and of the conduct of her son, whom Lafayette praised with the warmth of strong attachment. She listened calmly to him, and then replied, "*I am not surprised at what George has done, for he was always a very good boy.*" On leaving this venerable woman, Lafayette asked and received her blessing, and bade her a last farewell. When he took leave of Washington, he indulged a lively hope that they would once more meet; but when, in the year 1825, he again visited America, he was received as the "Nation's Guest," and, instead of being welcomed at Mount Vernon by Washington, he was led to his tomb to shed tears of sorrow.

CHAPTER XII.

SCARCELY had the sun of independence dawned on the United States,
when it was obscured by clouds. Common danger had kept them together,
while struggling for liberty, and almost without
a government. But that no longer existing,
the bonds that remained were too weak to
produce either unity of action or submission
to authority. A people who had just burst asunder
the shackles of a foreign government, were unwilling to impose upon themselves new fetters. The
states, which had acted in a great measure independent of each other during the war, were extremely unwilling to circumscribe their privileges, the
more dear for being but newly acquired; and a
large portion of the people shared in the sentiment.
It had become obvious that they could not long hold
together by the rope of sand of the confederation,
which left each one at liberty to reject or disregard

he requisitions of Congress. The enemies of li
berty had predicted the speedy dissolution of the
Union, and the prophecy seemed about to be fulfilled. People began to talk of the necessity of returning once more to the protection of England, or
establishing a kingly government. Washington, in
one of his letters, exclaims,—"What astonishing
changes a few years are capable of producing! I
am told that even respectable characters speak of a
monarchical form of government without horror!
From thinking proceeds speaking; thence to acting
is often but a single step. But how inexcusable and
tremendous! What a triumph for the advocates of
despotism to find that we are incapable of governing ourselves, and that systems founded on the basis
of equal liberty are merely ideal and fallacious!
Would to God that wise measures may be taken in
time to arrest the consequences we have so much
reason to apprehend! Retired as I am from the
world, I frankly acknowledge I cannot feel myself
an unconcerned spectator. Yet, having happily assisted in bringing the ship into port, and having
been fairly discharged, it is not my business to embark again on a sea of troubles." Yet he could not
desert his country in this new and perilous voyage
He employed the influence of his character, the

force of his reasonings, and the authority of his example, in producing a general impression of the absolute necessity of a modification of the government, to preserve its existence. He addressed letters to the governors of the states, and to the principal men of influence everywhere, urging them to come forward and lend their support to this indispensable measure. But it was a long time before even the authority and arguments of Washington could overcome the salutary fear with which every true lover of liberty contemplates an extension of authority.

The effect was, however, at length produced. Virginia took the lead, and she was the first to introduce a resolution for electing deputies to a General Convention for modifying the Articles of Confederation. An insurrection in Massachusetts, which occurred about this time, and which for a while baffled the authorities of the state, afforded additional proof of the utter weakness of the government, and demonstrated the necessity of a new organization. The name of Washington appeared at the head of the Virginia delegates, and he was urged on all sides, and with the most pressing arguments, to accept the appointment. Greatly as he oved Mount Vernon and the enjoyments of rural

life, he loved his country more. What he had laboured so earnestly to bring about in the beginning,
he could not and would not desert until it was
brought to an end, and, after long consideration, he
once more consented to return to public life. With
what unwillingness he made the sacrifice is seen in
various of his letters, wherein he expresses, with the
unaffected plainness of truth, his hesitation. Once
more he left his retirement, where, for a few short
years of his arduous existence, he had tasted the
blessings of a quiet and happy home.

On the second Monday in May, 1787, the Convention met at Philadelphia, and chose Washington
its president; and, after long and serious consultation on the important subject, that Constitution was
formed under which the United States have become
so prosperous, and the American nation so happy
and respectable. The opinions of the members of
the Convention seemed to be so opposed to each
other on some points, that it was feared they could
agree on no plan that would suit the whole country.
The debate was increasing in warmth, when Dr.
Franklin, with his accustomed wisdom and coolness.
endeavoured to promote harmony by proposing an
adjournment for three days, that there might be time

for serious consideration of the subject. He concluded this speech to the following effect:—

" The small progress we have made, after four or
five weeks' close attendance and continued reasoning
with each other, our different sentiments on almost
every question — several of the last producing as
many *noes* as *ayes* — is, methinks, a melancholy
proof of the imperfection of the human understanding. We, indeed, seem to *feel* our want of political
wisdom, since we have been running all about in
search of it. We have gone back to ancient history
for models of government, and examined the different forms of those republics which, having been
originally formed with the seeds of their own dissolution, now no longer exist: and we have viewed
modern states all round Europe, but find none of
their constitutions suitable to our circumstances.

" In this situation of this assembly, groping as it
were in the dark to find political truth, and scarcely
able to distinguish it when presented to us, how has
it happened, sir, that we have not hitherto once
thought of humbly applying to the Father of Light
to illuminate our understandings ?—In the beginning
of the contest with Britain, when we were sensible
of danger, we had daily prayers in this room for
Divine protection. Our prayers, sir, were heard ;—

and they were graciously answered. All of us, who were engaged in the struggle, must have observed frequent instances of a superintending Providence in our favour. To that kind Providence we owe this happy opportunity of consulting in peace on the means of establishing our future and national felicity. And have we now forgotten that powerful Friend? Or do we imagine we no longer need his assistance? I have lived, sir, a long time; and the longer I live, the more convincing proofs I see of this truth, *that God governs in the affairs of men.* And if a sparrow cannot fall to the ground without his notice, is it probable that an empire can rise without his aid? —We have been assured, sir, in the sacred writings, that 'except the Lord build the house, they labour in vain that build it.' I firmly believe this; and I also believe that, without his concurring aid, we shall succeed in this political building no better than the builders of Babel: we shall be divided by our little, partial, local interests; our projects will be confounded; and we ourselves shall become a reproach and a by-word down to future ages. And, what is worse, mankind may hereafter, from this unfortunate instance, despair of establishing governments by human wisdom, and leave it to chance, war, and conquest. I therefore beg leave to move—

" That henceforth prayers, imploring the assistance of Heaven, and its blessing on our deliberations, be made in this assembly every morning before we proceed to business ; and that one or more of the clergy of this city be requested to officiate in that service."

One member only opposed this motion, and a person who was present relates that, whilst he was making his objections, Washington fixed his eye upon him with an expression of mingled surprise and indignation. No one condescended to notice the opposition, and the proposal was at once carried by the votes of all the other members. The adjournment, also, according to his suggestion, took place, and, after the Convention had been opened with prayer, when they met again, Dr. Franklin stated the necessity and equity of mutual concessions from all parts of the Union. His views were adopted, and the important business, on which they were so warm when they separated, was soon despatched, and the whole constitution at length agreed to.

Under the new constitution, a chief magistrate became necessary to administer the government. The eyes of the people were at once directed to Washington, and their united voices called upon him, who had led their armies in war, to direct their affairs in peace. His old companions came forth and besought him to leave his retirement once more to serve his country. The leading men of all parties wrote letters to the same purport, and on all hands he was urged by the warmest, most earnest applications.

He was unanimously elected President of the United States on the fourth of March, 1789; but owing to some formal or accidental delays, this event was not notified to him officially until the fourteenth of April following. Referring to this delay, he thus expresses himself in a letter to General Knox, who possessed and deserved his friendship to the last moment of his life. "As to myself, the delay may be compared to a reprieve; for in confidence I tell you (with the world it would obtain little credit), that my movements towards the chair of government will be accompanied by feelings not unlike those of a culprit going to the place of execution; so unwilling am I, in the evening of a life consumed in public cares, to quit my peaceful abode for an ocean of difficulties, without the competency of political skill, abilities, and inclination which is necessary to manage the helm. I am sensible that I am embarking with the voice of the people, and a good name of my own, on this voyage; and what returns will be made for them, Heaven alone can foretell. Integrity and firmness are all I can promise. These, be the voyage long or short, shall never forsake me, though I may be deserted by all men; for of the consolations to be derived from these, the world cannot deprive me."

Such was the foundation of his modest confidence;—firmness and integrity, the true pillars of honest greatness. And these never deserted him. He kept his promise to himself in all times, circumstances, and temptations; and though, on a few rare occasions during the course of a stormy season, in which the hopes, fears, and antipathies of his fellow-citizens were strongly excited, his conduct may have been assailed, his motives were never questioned. None ever doubted his firmness, and the general conviction of his integrity was founded on a rock, that could neither be undermined nor overthrown.

Washington visited his mother to inform her of his appointment. He had endeavoured to prevail on her to make Mount Vernon the home of her latter years; but she would not consent to leave her humble dwelling, which was dear to her from having near it a rural spot, made private by surrounding rocks and trees, where she daily offered to her Crea tor her confessions and prayers. When her son told her he must bid her farewell, he said, "As soon as the weight of public business, which must necessarily attend the outset of a new government, can be disposed of, I shall return to Virginia, and"— "You will see me no more," said his mother, interrupting him; "my great age warns me, that I shall not be long in this world,—I trust in God that I may be somewhat prepared for a better. Go, George, go, my son! and perform your duties, and may the blessing of God, and that of a mother, be with you always." She put her arms around his neck, and, resting his head on the shoulder of his aged parent, the truly great man shed tears of filial tenderness. He parted from her with the sad feeling that he should indeed see her no more, and in a short time these painful apprehensions were realized.

His progress from Mount Vernon to New York, where Congress was then sitting, was a succession of the most affecting scenes which the sentiment of a grateful people ever presented to the contemplation of the world. His appearance awakened in the bosoms of all an enthusiasm, so much the more glorious because little characteristic of our countrymen. Men, women, and children poured forth and lined the roads in throngs to see him pass, and hail his coming; the windows shone with glistening eyes, watching his passing footsteps; the women wept for joy; the children shouted, "God save Washington!" and the hearts of the stout husbandmen yearned with affection toward him who had caused them to repose in safety under their own vine and their own fig-tree. His old companions in arms came forth to renovate their honest pride, as well as undying affection, by a sight of their general, and a shake of his hand. The pulse of the nation beat high with exultation; for now, when they saw their ancient pilot once more at the helm, they hoped for a prosperous voyage and a quiet haven in the bosom of prosperity.

His reception at Trenton was peculiarly touching. It was planned by those females and their daughters whose patriotism and sufferings, in the cause of liberty, were equal to those of their fathers, husbands, sons, and brothers. It was here, when the hopes of the people lay prostrate on the earth, and the eagle of freedom seemed to flap his wings, as if preparing to forsake the world, that Washington had performed those prompt and daring acts which, while they revived the drooping spirits of his country, freed, for a time, the matrons of Trenton from the insults and wrongs of an arrogant soldiery. The female heart is no sanctuary for ingratitude; and when Washington arrived at the bridge over the Assumpink, which here flows close to the borders of the city, he met the sweetest reward that perhaps ever crowned his virtues. Over the bridge was thrown an arch of evergreens and flowers, bearing this inscription in large letters:—

" December 26, 1776.
" *The hero who defended the mothers will protect the daughters.*"

At the other extremity of the bridge were assembled many hundred girls, of various ages, arrayed in white, the emblem of truth and innocence, their brows circled with garlands, and baskets of flowers in their hands. Beyond these were disposed the grown-up daughters of the land, clothed and equipped like the others,—and behind them the matrons, all of whom remembered the never to be forgotten twenty-sixth of December, 1776. As he left the bridge, they joined in a chorus, touchingly expressive of his services and their gratitude, strewing at the same time flowers as he passed along.

His reception everywhere was worthy of his services, and of a grateful people. At New York, the vessels were adorned with flags, and the river alive with boats, gayly decked out in like manner, with bands of music on board; the place of his landing was thronged with crowds of citizens, gathered together to welcome his arrival. The roar of cannon and the shouts of the multitude announced his landing, and he was conducted to his lodging by thousands of grateful hearts, who remembered what he had done for them in the days of their trial. It had been arranged that a military escort should attend him; but when the officer in command announced his commission, Washington replied, " I require no guard but the affections of the people," and declined their attendance.

At this moment, Washington, though grateful for these spontaneous proofs of affectionate veneration, was not elated. In describing the scene in one of his familiar letters, he says :—" The display of boats on this occasion, with vocal and instrumental music on board, the decorations of the ships, the roar of cannon, and the loud acclamations of the people, as I passed along the wharves, gave me as much pain as pleasure, contemplating the probable reversal of this scene, after all my endeavours to do good." Happily, his anticipations were never realized. Although his policy in relation to the French Revolution, which was as wise as it was happy in its consequences, did not give universal satisfaction, still he remained master of the affections and confidence of the people. The laurels he had won in defence of the liberties of his country, continued to flourish on his brow while living, and will grow green on his grave to the end of time.

On the thirtieth day of April, 1789, he took the oath, and entered on the office of President of the United States, one of the highest as well as most thankless that could be undertaken by man. The head of this free government is no idle, empty pageant, set up to challenge the admiration, and coerce the absolute submission of the people; his duties are arduous, and his responsibilities great; he is the first servant, not the master of the state, and is amenable for his conduct, like the humblest citizen. As the executor of the laws, he is bound to see them obeyed; as the first of our citizens, he is equally bound to set an example of obedience. The oath, "to preserve, protect, and defend the constitution of the United States," was administered in the balcony of the old Federal Hall in New York, by the chancellor of the state, and the interesting ceremony was witnessed by a great concourse of people. All stood in silence, until the oath was taken, and then,

when the Chancellor proclaimed that GEORGE WASH-
INGTON WAS THE PRESIDENT OF THE UNITED STATES,
a shout of joy burst from many thousands of grateful and affectionate hearts. The president went into
the senate chamber, and in a modest but dignified
manner, addressed the senate and house of repre
sentatives. In the course of his address he said,—
" It will be peculiarly improper to omit, in this first
official act, my fervent supplications to that Almighty
Being, who rules over the universe,—who presides
in the councils of nations, and whose providential
aid can supply every human defect,—that his benediction may consecrate to the liberties and happiness of the people of the United States, a government instituted by themselves for these essential
purposes,—and may enable every instrument employed in its administration to execute with success
the functions allotted to his charge. In tendering
this homage to the great Author of every public
and private good, I assure myself that it expresses
your sentiments not less than my own; nor those
of my fellow-citizens at large, less than either. No
people can be bound to acknowledge and adore
the invisible hand which conducts the affairs of men,
more than the people of the United States. Every
step by which they have advanced to the character

THE INAUGURATION OF PRESIDENT WASHINGTON.　Page 162.

of an independent nation, seems to have been distinguished by some token of providential agency."
In conclusion, he said, " I shall take my present
leave, but not without resorting once more to the
benign Parent of the human race, in humble suppli-
cation, that since he has been pleased to favour the
American people with opportunities for deliberating
in perfect tranquillity, and dispositions for deciding,
with unparalleled unanimity, on a form of government for the security of their union and advance-
ment of their happiness; so his divine blessing may
be equally conspicuous in the enlarged views, the
temperate consultations, and wise measures, on which
the success of this government must depend."

The Senate, in reply, expressed their high estima-
tion of his wisdom and virtue, and said, " All that
remains is that we join in your fervent supplications
for the blessing of Heaven on our country; and that
we add our own for the choicest of those blessings
on the most beloved of her citizens."

CHAPTER XIII.

THE administration of Washington— extending from 1789 to 1797—was as honourable as had been his military life. There were difficulties enough, in the formation of a new government like ours, to test the wisdom and the patriotism of the greatest of men; but the condition of the world at this period of almost universal up-turnings and overthrows, rendered the direction of public affairs doubly arduous and perilous. The Father of his Country seemed now, as he had seemed when at the head of our armies, the liberating and guiding minister of the King of kings.

As when in the field, Washington declined receiving from the people anything beyond his actual expenditures. He called round him a cabinet of the most able and honest statesmen, and with them devoted himself incessantly to the arduous business of putting the government in successful operation

Among the subjects which engaged his earnest consideration was the situation of the inland frontier,
now exposed to the inroads and revenge of the Indians. His policy, with regard to these unfortunate
people, was successful in quieting, if not conciliating
many of them ; but others remained refractory, and
continued their atrocities.   After defeating two
American armies, with great slaughter, they were
at length brought to terms by General Wayne, who
gave them so severe an overthrow, in a general
action, that they sued for peace. This was concluded
at Greenville; and the cession of a vast territory, not
only relieved the frontier from savage inroads, but
paved the way for the progress of civilization into
a new world of wilderness.

He was equally successful at a subsequent period
in his negotiations with Spain. His high character
gave him great advantages in his foreign intercourse. He proceeded in a straightforward manner; stated what was wanted, and what would be
given in return ; relied on justice, and enforced its
claims with the arguments of truth. He disdained
to purchase advantages by corruption, or to deceive
by insincerity. As in private, he proceeded upon
the maxim, every day verified, that " Honesty is the
best policy." The conviction of a man's integrity

gives him greater advantages in intercourse with the world than he can gain by hypocrisy and falsehood.

The settlement of the controversies growing out of the treaty with England proved even more difficult than those with Spain. The wounds inflicted on both nations by a war of so many years were healed, but the scars remained, to remind the one of what it had suffered, the other of what it had lost. Time and mutual good offices were necessary to allay that spirit which had been excited on one hand by injuries, on the other by successful resistance; and time indeed had passed away, but it had left behind it neither forgiveness nor oblivion. It was accompanied on one hand by new provocations, on the other by additional remonstrances and renewed indignation. Negotiations continued for a long while, without any result but mortification and impatience on the part of the people of the United States; and it was not until the French Revolution threatened the existence of all the established governments of Europe, and England among the rest, that a treaty was concluded, which brought with it an adjustment of the principal points that had so long embroiled the two nations, and fostered a spirit of increasing hostility. The most vexing question of all, however, that of the right of entering our ships and impressing seamen, was left unsettled, and it became obvious that it would never be adjusted except on the principle of the right of the strongest. About the same time, peace was concluded between the United States and the Emperor of Morocco, and thus, for a while, our commerce remained unmolested on that famous sea, where, some years afterwards, our gallant navy laid the foundation of its present and future glories.

The commencement and progress of the French revolution occasioned the first and bitterest division of parties in the United States. The people of the United States had continued to cherish a strong feeling of gratitude for the good offices of France during their struggle for independence; and in addition to this, their sympathies were deeply engaged in behalf of a contest so similar in many respects to their own. The institution of the French republic was hailed with an enthusiasm equal to that they felt on the establishment of their own liberties. Washington himself did not hesitate to avow his kindly feelings and wishes for the liberal party in France, at first; but when the reign of terror set in, and the order of Jacobins was established, he contemplated the scene with horror, as did every intelligent and

true-hearted friend of liberty throughout the world.
In one of his public papers, in 1783, he had said
that " there is a natural and necessary progression
from the extreme of anarchy to the extreme of
tyranny ;" and that " arbitrary power is most easily
established on the ruins of liberty abused to licen-
tiousness." A few years afterwards he saw that
these maxims were to be verified in the case of
France. The result justified the caution with which
he avoided an alliance with that power. But independent of the powerful reasons for neutrality, he
knew that peace was indispensable to the United
States in the infancy of their national existence and
affairs. He issued his proclamation of neutrality,
from which Mr. Genet, the minister of the French
republic, threatened to appeal to the people, a measure understood to mean nothing less than revolution. From that moment the people began to rally
around their beloved chief, like children who will
not allow their father to be insulted, although they
themselves may think him wrong. They sanctioned
the proclamation, and time has ratified their decision.

In 1794, after Washington had been a second
time elected to the presidency, he had occasion to
exhibit his wisdom and his firmness in the suppres-
sion of the insurrection in the western part of Penn

sylvania. Congress had imposed a tax on spirits distilled within the United States, and some of the inhabitants of that part of the country, not only refused to pay the tax, but treated with violence those who were appointed to collect it. The disgraceful example was followed by so many, that it became necessary for the president to notice it. He endeavoured to make the insurgents submit quietly to the laws, but when he found they would not do so, he determined on sending against them a force which would be too powerful to resist. By doing this, he hoped to prevent any bloodshed. Troops were directed to assemble at Bedford, and at Cumberland, on the Potomac. Governor Lee, of Virginia, was appointed to command the expedition, and as had been anticipated, the greatness of the force subdued, without the actual use of arms, the misguided enemies of the law.

While he was deeply engaged in public business, he heard that Lafayette had been driven from his native land, by the unprincipled men who were conducting the revolution there ; and that he had been seized in Prussia, and sent to Austria , the emperor of which country directed that he should be confined in a dungeon, in the town of Olmutz. Washington could not interfere for his release, except in the private character of a friend ; but he used every means in his power to obtain it, and wrote a letter to the emperor of Austria, requesting him to permit Lafayette to come to America. But his request was not granted. Bolman, a young German, and a young American named Huger, formed a plan for effecting his escape. He was sometimes permitted to leave his dungeon, and walk a short distance with a guard. One day Bolman and Huger watched for him, having a horse ready, which Huger led suddenly up to him, and desired him to mount ; the horse was frightened and ran off, Bolman followed to endeavour to catch it, and Huger then insisted that Lafayette should accept his horse, which he did, and was soon out of sight. Bolman could not overtake the affrighted horse, and he returned and took Huger behind him, and they followed the freed prisoner. The guard gave the alarm, and they were quickly pursued ; Huger was seized, but Bolman at that time escaped. Lafayette was stopped, and brought back to Olmutz. Chained, hand and foot, Huger was carried before a judge, who told him that it was probable his life would be the forfeit of his attempt to assist Lafayette to escape ; but that possibly the emperor would treat him with clemency, on account of his youth and motives. " Clemency !"

said Huger, " how can I expect it from a man who did not act even with justice to Lafayette ?" The judge said to him, " If ever I need a friend, I hope that friend may be an American." Huger suffered from a close imprisonment for some time, and was then allowed to return to his own country.

The efforts of Washington for the release of his friend, did not cease, however, and perhaps the letter which he wrote to the emperor had the effect of lessening the severity with which he was treated, and of shortening the period of his captivity. His son, named George Washington, escaped from France, and arrived at Boston. The president advised him to enter the University at Cambridge, and assured him that he would stand in the place of a father to him, and become his friend, protector, and supporter.

When the time came for a third election of president, the people were again ready to unite in voting for Washington. But he firmly refused to be re-elected. He assured his countrymen that he did not do so from any want of respect for their past kindness, or from feeling less anxious for their future prosperity ; — that he had twice yielded to their wishes, because he thought that it was his duty to do so, but felt that then the happy state of their concerns would permit his retiring to enjoy the quiet of his own home. As his determination was firm, they did not persist in opposing it, and he prepared to take again the character of a private citizen. In concluding his last speech to Congress, he said, "I cannot omit the occasion to repeat my fervent supplications to the Supreme Ruler of the universe and sovereign arbiter of nations, that his providential care may still be extended to the United States; that the virtue and happiness of the people may be preserved, and that the government, which they have instituted for the protection of their liberties, may be perpetual."

He also published a farewell address to the people of the United States, which contains the most instructive, important, and interesting advice, that was ever given to any nation. He was now about to withdraw his long and salutary guardianship from this young and vigorous country, his only offspring, and he left her the noblest legacy in his power, the priceless riches of his precepts and example.

"In looking forward," he says, "to the moment which is intended to terminate the career of my public life, my feelings do not permit me to suspend the deep acknowledgment of that debt of gratitude which I owe to my beloved country for the many honours it has conferred upon me, or still more for the steadfast confidence with which it has supported me, and for the opportunities thence enjoyed of manifesting my inviolable attachment by services useful and persevering, though in usefulness unequal to my zeal.

"Profoundly penetrated with this idea, I shall carry it with me to my grave, as a strong incitement to unceasing vows, that Heaven may continue to you the choicest tokens of its beneficence; that your union and brotherly affection may be perpetual; that the free constitution which is the work of your hands may be sacredly maintained; that its administration in every department may be stamped with wisdom and virtue; that in fine, the happiness of these States, under the auspices of liberty, may be made complete by so careful a preservation, and so prudent a use of this blessing, as will acquire to them the glory of recommending it to the applause, the affection, and the adoption of every nation which is yet a stranger to it.

"Here, perhaps, I ought to stop. But solicitude for your welfare, which cannot end but with my life, and the apprehension of danger natural to such solicitude, urge me, on an occasion like the present, to offer to your solemn contemplation, and to recommend to your frequent review, some sentiments which are the result of much reflection, of no inconsiderable observation, and which appear to me all-important to your felicity as a people. These will be offered to you with the more freedom, as you can only see in them the disinterested warnings of a parting friend, who can possibly have no personal motive to bias his counsel.

"Interwoven as is the love of liberty with every ligament of your hearts, no recommendation of mine is necessary to fortify the attachment.

"The unity of government, which constitutes you one people, is also now dear to you. It is justly so; for it is the main pillar in the edifice of your real independence, the support of your tranquillity at home and your peace abroad; of your prosperity, of that liberty which you so highly prize. But as it is easy to foresee that from different causes and from different quarters, much pains will be taken, many artifices employed, to weaken in your minds the conviction of this truth, (as this is the point in your political fortress against which the batteries of internal and external enemies will be constantly and actively, though often covertly and insidiously directed,) it is of infinite moment that you should properly estimate the immense value of your national union to your collective and individual happiness; that you should cherish a cordial, habitual, and immoveable attachment to it, accustoming yourselves to think and speak of it as of the palladium of your political safety and prosperity; watching for its preservation with jealous anxiety; discountenancing whatever may suggest even a suspicion that it may in any event be abandoned; and indignantly frowning upon every attempt to alienate any portion of our country from the rest, or to enfeeble the sacred ties that now link together the various parts."

He then proceeds to caution his fellow-citizens against those geographical distinctions of *North, South, East,* and *West,* which, by fostering ideas of separate interests and character, are calculated to weaken the bonds of our union, and to create prejudices, if not antipathies, dangerous to its existence. He shows, by a simple reference to the great paramount interests of each of the different sections, that they are inseparably intertwined in one common bond; that they are mutually dependent on each other; and that they cannot be rent asunder without deeply wounding our prosperity at home, our character and influence abroad, laying the foundation for perpetual broils among ourselves, and creating a necessity for great standing armies, themselves the most fatal enemies to the liberties of mankind.

He earnestly recommends implicit obedience to the laws of the land, as one of the great duties enjoined by the fundamental maxims of liberty. "The basis of our political system," he says, "is the right of the people to make and alter their constitutions of government; but the constitution which at any time exists, till changed by an explicit and authentic act of the whole people, is sacredly obligatory upon all. The very idea of the power and right of the people to establish government, presupposes the duty of every individual to obey the established government."

He denounces "all combinations and associations under whatever plausible character, with the real design to direct, control, counteract, or awe the regular deliberation and action of the constituted authorities," as destructive to this fundamental principle and of fatal tendency. He cautions his countrymen against the extreme excitements of party spirit; the factious opposition and pernicious excesses to which they inevitably tend, until by degrees they gradually incline the minds of men to seek security and repose in the absolute power of an individual; and sooner or later the chief of some prevailing faction, more able or more fortunate than his competitors, turns this disposition to the purposes of his own elevation, on the ruins of public liberty.

He warns those who are to administer the government after him, "to confine themselves within their respective constitutional spheres, refraining, in the exercise of the powers of one department, to encroach upon another. The spirit of encroachment tends to consolidate the powers of all the departments in one, and thus to create, whatever the form of government, real despotism."

He inculcates, with the most earnest eloquence, a regard to religion and morality.

"Of all the dispositions and habits," he says "which lead to political prosperity, religion and morality are indispensable supports. In vain would that man claim the tribute of patriotism who should labour to subvert these great pillars of human happiness, these firmest props of men and citizens. The mere politician, equally with the pious man, ought to respect and to cherish them. A volume could not trace all their connections with private and public felicity. Let it be simply added, where is the security for property, for reputation for life, if the sense of religious obligation desert the oaths

M

which are the instruments of investigation in courts
of justice?. And let us with caution indulge the
supposition that morality can be attained without
religion. Whatever may be conceded to a refined
education, or minds of peculiar cast, reason and
experience both forbid us to expect that national
morality can prevail in the exclusion of religious
principles."

He recommends the general diffusion of know-
.edge among all classes of the people. " Promote,
then," he says, " as an object of primary importance,
institutions for the general diffusion of knowledge
In proportion as the structure of government gives
force to public opinion, it is essential that public
opinion should be enlightened."

He recommends the practice of justice and good
faith, and the cultivation of the relations of peace
with all mankind, as not only enforced by the obliga-
tions of religion and morality, but by all the maxims
of sound policy. For the purpose of a successful
pursuit of this great object, he cautions his fellow-
citizens against the indulgence of undue partiality
or prejudice in favour or against any nation whatever, as leading to weak sacrifices on one hand,
senseless hostility on the other.

Most emphatically does he warn them against the

wiles of foreign influence, the fatal enemy of all the ancient republics. He enjoins a watchful jealousy of all equally impartial, otherwise it may only lead to the suspicion of visionary dangers on one hand, and wilful blindness on the other. Then, after recommending a total abstinence from all *political* alliances with the nations of Europe; a due regard to the national faith towards public creditors; suitable establishments for the defence of the country, that we may not be tempted to rely on foreign aid, which will never be afforded, in all probability, without the price of great sacrifices on the part of the nation depending on the hollow friendship of jealous rivals, he concludes this admirable address, which ought to be one of the early lessons of every youth of our country, in the following affecting words :—

"Though in reviewing the incidents of my administration, I am unconscious of intentional error, I am nevertheless too sensible of my defects, not to think it probable that I may have committed many errors. Whatever they may be, I fervently beseech the Almighty to avert or mitigate the evils to which they may tend. I shall always carry with me the hope that my country will never cease to view them with indulgence, and that after forty-five years of a life dedicated to its service, with an upright zeal, the faults of incompetent abilities will be consigned to oblivion, as myself must soon be to the mansions of rest.

" Relying on its kindness in this as in all other things, and actuated by that fervent love towards it, which is so natural to a man who views it as the native soil of himself and his progenitors for several generations, I anticipate with pleasing expectations that retreat in which I promise myself to realize, without alloy, the sweet enjoyment of partaking in the midst of my fellow-citizens the benign influence of good laws under a free government, the ever favourite object of my heart, and the happy reward, as I trust, of our mutual cares, labours, and dan gers."

CHAPTER XIV.

HE long, and anxiously ant'cipated period, at length came, wnen the greatest of men might quietly repose under the shadow of that tree of Liberty, which he himself had planted in a soil enriched with the blood of her sons. Mount Vernon became no scene of luxurious ease, for the active habits which Washington had formed in the field and in the cabinet were still preserved. But the sword was exchanged for implements of husbandry, and the parade and circumstance of power for the quiet and unostentatious enjoyments of domestic life. Mount Vernon became the Mecca of freemen, who thronged its hospitable doors from all parts of Christendom. The ministers of foreign nations paid first their respects to the president incumbent, and then bent their steps to the peaceful and glorious retirement of the man who had given a new impulse to humanity, and whose name had become a word of hope to the enslaved and down trodden in the remotest empires. Philosophers, and statesmen, and men of letters came to converse with the nearest approach to a *faultless man* which the world has furnished. His old companions in arms, too, were frequent and welcome visitors, with whom he delighted to live over again the days of suffering or of triumph through which they had passed. He wore now, by the assent of the world, the triple wreath, which never had been worn so worthily by other man, of Hero, Patriot and Sage.

Washington's manners were at all times dignified, but the most humble citizen had never more simplicity. One day, after his return to his farm, he was visited by Colonel Meade, an old friend, who, meeting Mr. Custis, a relative of Mrs. Washington, at the mansion, inquired of him where he could see the General. Mr. Custis, not knowing Colonel Meade, replied, that Washington was out; and, giving directions as to the part of the farm on which he would probably be found, added, " You will meet, sir, with an *old gentleman, riding alone, in plain drab clothes, a broad-brimmed white hat, a hickory switch in his hand, and carrying an umbrella, with a long staff, which is attached to his saddle-bow: that sir, is General Washington.*" Colonel Meade replied,

"Thank you, thank you, young gentleman; I think if I fall in with the General, I shall be apt to know him."

This anecdote will give an idea of Washington's appearance at this period, but we may here give a more accurate description of his person, by Mr Custis, who was with him constantly in the last days of his life. His great physical powers, so remarkable in his maturity, were in his limbs, which were long, large, and sinewy. His frame was of equal breadth from the shoulders to the hips. His chest, though broad and expansive, was not prominent, but rather hollowed in the centre. He had suffered from a pulmonary affection in early life, from which he never entirely recovered. His frame showed an extraordinary development of bone and muscle; his joints were large, as were his feet; and could a cast have been preserved of his hand, to be exhibited in these degenerate days, it would be said to have belonged to the being of a fabulous age. During the last visit of Lafayette to Mount Vernon, among many, and interesting relations of events that occurred in olden days, he said to Mr. Custis: "It was in this portico that you were introduced to me in 1784; you were then holding by a single finger of

the good General's remarkable hand, which was all
that you could do, my dear sir, at that time."

In the various exhibitions of Washington's physical prowess, they were apparently attended by
scarcely any effort.   When he overthrew the strong
man of Virginia in wrestling, while many of the
young athletæ of the times were engaged in the
manly games, Washington had retired to the shade
of a tree, intent upon the perusal of a favourite
volume; and it was only when the champion of the
games strode through the ring, calling for nobler
competitors, and taunting the student with the reproach that it • was the fear of encountering so
redoubted an antagonist that kept him from the ring,
that Washington closed his book, and without divest-
ing himself of his coat, calmly walked into the arena,
observing that fear formed no part of his being; then
grappling with the champion, the struggle was fierce
but momentary, "for," said the vanquished hero of the
arena, " in Washington's iron-like grasp, I became
powerless and was hurled to the ground, with a force
that seemed to jar the very marrow in my bones;
while the victor, regardless of the shouts that proclaimed his triumph, leisurely retired to his shade,
and enjoyment of his favourite volume."

The power of Washington's arm was displayed

in several memorable instances ; as in his throwing a
stone across the Rappahannock river, below Fred-
ericksburg, another from the bed of the stream to
the top of the Natural Bridge, and yet another over
the Palisades into the Hudson.   While C. H. Peale,
the well-known artist, was at Mount Vernon in 1772,
engaged in painting the portrait of the provincial
Colonel, some of the young men were contending
in the exercise of pitching the bar.   Washington
looked on for a time, then grasping the missile in his
master hand, whirled the iron through the air, which
took the ground far, very far, beyond its former
limits—the Colonel observing with a smile, " You
perceive, young gentlemen, that my arm yet retains
some portion of the vigour of my earlier days."   He
was then in his fortieth year, and probably in the full
meridian of his physical powers ; but those powers
became rather mellowed than decayed by time, for
" his age was like a lusty winter, frostly, yet kindly.
and up to his sixty-eighth year, he mounted a horse
with surprising agility, and rode with the ease and
gracefulness of his better days.   His personal
prowess that elicited the admiration of a people who
have nearly all passed from the stage of life, still
serves as a model for the manhood of modern times.

   With all its development of muscular power, the

form of **Washington** had no appearance of bulkiness, and so harmonious were its proportions that he did not appear so passing tall as his portraits have represented. He was rather spare than full during his whole life; this is readily ascertained from his weight. The last time he was weighed was in the summer of 1799, when having made the tour of his farms, accompanied by an English gentleman, he called at his mill for this purpose. Mr. Custis placed the weight in the scales. The Englishman, not so tall, but stout, square-built, and fleshy, weighed heavily, and expressed much surprise that the General had not outweighed him, when Washington observed, that the best weight of his best days never exceeded from 210 to 220. In the instance now alluded to, he weighed a little more than 210.

The portraits of **Washington** generally give to his person a fulness that it did not possess, together with an abdominal enlargement greater than in the life, while his matchless limbs have in but two instances been faithfully portrayed: in the equestrian portrait by Trumbull of 1790, a copy of which is in the City Hall of New York, and in an engraving by Loisler, from a painting by Cogniet, French artists of distinguished merit. The latter is not an original painting, the head being from Stuart, but the delineation of the limbs is the most perfect extant.

Of the remarkable degree of awe and reverence which the presence of Washington always inspired, we shall give but one out of a thousand instances. During the cantonment of the American army at the Valley Forge, some officers of the 4th Pennsylvania regiment were engaged in a game of fives. In the midst of their sport they discovered the Commander-in-Chief leaning upon the enclosure and beholding the game with evident satisfaction. In a moment all things were changed. The ball was suffered to roll idle away, the gay laugh and joyous shout of excitement were hushed into a profound silence, and the officers were gravely grouped together. It was in vain the chief begged of the players they would proceed with their game, declared the pleasure he had in witnessing their skill, and spoke of a proficiency in the manly exercise which he himself could have boasted of in other days. All would not do. Not a man could be induced to move, till the General, finding that his presence hindered the officers from continuing the amusement, bowed, and, wishing them good sport, retired.

Another anecdote, not unlike the foregoing, is related by Mr. Paulding.

" When Washington retired from public life, his name and fame excited in the hearts of the people at large, and most especially of the more youthful portion, a degree of reverence which, by checking their vivacity or awing them into silence, often gave him great pain. Being once on a visit to Colonel Blackburn, a large company of young people were assembled to welcome his arrival, or on some other festive occasion. Washington was unusually cheerful and animated, but he observed that whenever he made his appearance, the dance lost its vivacity, the little gossipings in corners ceased, and a solemn silence prevailed, as at the presence of one they either feared or reverenced too much to permit them to enjoy themselves. He strove to remove this restraint by mixing familiarly among them and talking with unaffected hilarity. But it was all in vain; there was a spell on the little circle, and he retired among the elders in an adjoining room, appearing to be much pained at the restraint his presence inspired. When, however, the young people had again become animated, he arose cautiously from his seat, walked on tiptoe to the door, which was ajar, and stood contemplating the scene for nearly a quarter of an hour, with a look of genuine and

benevolent pleasure that went to the very hearts of
the parents who were observing him."

The days of Washington were spent in usefu
employments, and his evenings in the enjoyment of
domestic happiness. It was his custom to read to
his family such new publications as interested him,
and on Sunday evenings the Bible and a sermon.
Sometimes he would sit, as if he forgot that he was
not alone, and raising his hand, would move his lips
silently, as if engaged in prayer. In town or country, he was a constant attendant upon public worship,
and by his devout deportment there, proved that he
went there for the purpose of worshipping God.
He always acknowledged by his example, that he
felt his solemn obligation to keep holy the Sabbath
day; and to influence others to do so as far as was
within his power.

.

CHAPTER XV.

E come now to the last chapter in the history of Washington—to the last scene of his glorious life in this world, which he left but to join the immortal company of great and good in Heaven. Mr. Bushrod Washington, one of his nephews, visited him a few days before his death. "During this visit to the General," he says, " we walked together about the grounds, and talked of various improvements he had in contemplation. The lawn was to be extended down to the river in the direction of the old vault, which was to be removed on account of the inroads made by the roots of the trees, with which it is crowned, which caused it to leak. 'I intend to place it there,' said he pointing to the spot where the new vault now stands 'First of all, I shall make this change; for, after all I may require it before the rest.'

' When I parted from him, he stood on the steps of the front door, where he took leave of myself and another, and wished us a pleasant journey, as I was going to Westmoreland on business. It was a bright frosty morning, he had taken his usual ride, and the clear healthy flush on his cheek, and his sprightly manner, brought the remark from both of us that we had never seen the General look so well. I have sometimes thought him decidedly the handsomest man I ever saw; and when in a lively mood, so full of pleasantry, so agreeable to all with whom he associated, that I could hardly realize that he was the same Washington whose dignity awed all who approached him. A few days after, being on my return home in company with others, while we were conversing about Washington, I saw a servant rapidly riding towards us. On his near approach, I recognised him as belonging to Mount Vernon. He rode up—his countenance told the story—he handed me a letter. Washington was dead!"

The most authentic and most interesting account of this melancholy event, is given by Tobias Lear, one of his attendants, who drew up the following statement, on the day after its occurrence. We have no fear that our readers will think the details too particular.

" On Thursday, December 12th, the General rode out to his farm at about ten o'clock, and did not return home till past three. Soon after he went out the weather became very bad; rain, hail, and snow falling alternately, with a cold wind. When ne came in, I carried some letters to him to frank, intending to send them to the post-office. He franked the letters, but said the weather was too bad to send a servant to the office that evening. I observed to him that I was afraid he had got wet; he said no— his great-coat had kept him dry; but his neck appeared to be wet—the snow was hanging to his hair.

" He came to dinner without changing his dress. In the evening he appeared as well as usual. A heavy fall of snow took place on Friday, which prevented the General from riding out as usual. He had taken cold, (undoubtedly from being so much exposed the day before,) and complained of having a sore throat; he had a hoarseness, which increased in the evening, but he made light of it, as he would never take anything to carry off a cold,—always observing, "let it go as it came." In the evening, the papers having come from the post-office, he sat in the room, with Mrs. Washington and myself, reading them, till about nine o'clock; and, when he met with anything which he thought diverting or interesting, he would read it aloud. He desired me to read to him the debates of the Virginia Assembly, on the election of a senator and governor, which I did. On his retiring to bed, he appeared to be in perfect health, except the cold, which he considered as trifling—he had been remarkably cheerful all the evening.

"About two or three o'clock on Saturday morning, he awoke Mrs. Washington, and informed her he was very unwell, and had an ague. She observed that he could scarcely speak, and breathed with difficulty, and she wished to get up and call a servant; but the General would not permit her, lest she should take cold. As soon as the day appeared, the woman Caroline went into the room to make a fire, and the girl desired that Mr. Rawlins, one of the overseers, who was used to bleeding the people, might be sent for to bleed him before the Doctor could arrive. I was sent for—went to the General's chamber, where Mrs. Washington was up, and related to me his being taken ill between two and three o'clock, as before stated. I found him breathing with difficulty, and hardly able to utter a word intelligibly. I went out instantly, and wrote a line to Dr. Plask, and sent it with all speed. Immediately

N

I returned to the General's chamber, where I found him in the same situation I had left him. A mixture of molasses, vinegar and butter, was prepared, but he could not swallow a drop; whenever he attempted it he was distressed, convulsed, and almost suffocated.

"Mr. Rawlins came in soon after sunrise, and prepared to bleed him; when the arm was ready, the General observing Rawlins appeared agitated, said, with difficulty, "don't be afraid;" and, after the incision was made, he observed the orifice was not large enough—however the blood ran pretty freely. Mrs. Washington, not knowing whether bleeding was proper in the General's situation, begged that much blood might not be taken from him, and desired me to stop it. When I was about to untie the string, the General put up his hand to prevent it, and, so soon as he could speak, said " more."

"Mrs. Washington being still uneasy lest too much blood should be taken, it was stopped, after about half a pint had been taken. Finding that no relief could be obtained from bleeding, and that nothing could be swallowed, I proposed bathing the throat externally with sal volatile, which was done; a piece of flannel was then put around his neck. His feet were also soaked in warm water, but it gave no relief. By Mrs. Washington's request, I des

patched a messenger for Dr. Brown, at Port To-
bacco. About 9 o'clock Dr. Craik arrived, and put
a blister of flies on the throat of the General, and
took more blood, and had some vinegar and hot
water set in a teapot for him to draw in the steam
from the spout.

"He also had sage tea and vinegar mixed and
used as a gargle; but, when he held back his head
to let it run down, it almost produced suffocation.
When the mixture came out of his mouth some
phlegm followed it, and he would attempt to cough,
which the Doctor encouraged, but without effect.
About eleven o'clock, Dr. Dick was sent for. Dr.
Craik bled the General again, but no effect was produced, and he continued in the same state, unable to
swallow anything. Dr. Dick came in about three
o'clock, and Dr. Brown arrived soon after; when,
after consultation, the General was bled again, the
blood ran slowly, appeared very thick, and did not
produce any symptoms of fainting. At four o'clock
the General could swallow a little. Calomel and
tartar emetic were administered without effect.
About half past four o'clock he desired me to ask
Mrs. Washington to come to his bedside, when he
desired her to go down to his room and take from
his desk two wills which she would find there, and

bring them to him, which she did; upon looking at one, which he observed was useless, he desired her to burn it, which she did, and then took the other and put it away; after this was done, I returned again to his bedside and took his hand: he said to me, " I find I am going—my breath cannot continue long: I believed from the first attack it would be fatal. Do you arrange and record all my military letters and papers ; arrange my accounts and settle my books, as you know more about them than any one else; and let Mr. Rawlins finish recording my other letters, which he has begun." He asked when Mr. Lewis and Washington would return? I told him I believed about the 20th of the month. He made no reply to it.

" The physicians came in between five and six o'clock, and, when they came to his bedside, Dr. Craik asked him if he would sit up in the bed: he held out his hand to me and was raised up, when he said to the physician—" I feel myself going ; you had better not take any more trouble about me, but let me go off quietly ; I cannot last long." They found what had been done was without effect: he laid down again, and they retired, excepting Dr. Craik He then said to him—" Doctor, I die hard, but I am not afraid to go ; I believed, from my first

THE DEATH OF WASHINGTON.   Page 196.

attack, I should not survive it; my breath cannot last long." The doctor pressed his hand, but could not utter a word; he retired from the bedside and sat by the fire, absorbed in grief. About eight o'clock the physicians again came into the room, and applied blisters to his legs, but went out without a ray of hope. From this time he appeared to breathe with less difficulty than he had done, but was very restless, continually changing his position, to endeavour to get ease. I aided him all in my power, and was gratified in believing he felt it, for he would look upon me with eyes speaking gratitude, but unable to utter a word without great distress. About ten o'clock he made several attempts to speak to me before he could effect it; at length he said, " I am just going. Have me decently buried; and do not let my body be put into the vault in less than two days after I am dead." I bowed assent. He looked at me again, and said, " Do you understand me?" I replied, " Yes, sir." " 'T is well," said he. About ten minutes before he expired, his breathing became much easier—he lay quietly—he withdrew his hand from mine, and felt his own pulse. I spoke to Dr. Craik, who sat by the fire; he came to the bedside. The General's hand fell from his wrist; I took it in mine and placed it on my breast. Dr

Craik placed his hands over his eyes, and he expired without a struggle or a sigh. His loved wife kneeled beside his bed, with her head resting on the Bible, in which she daily read the precepts and cheering promises of her Saviour; and they comforted her in her hour of deepest sorrow. Her miniature portrait was found on the bosom of Washington, where he had worn it for forty years."

The report of his death reached Congress before they knew of his illness. When they heard it, a solemn silence prevailed for several minutes; John Marshall, afterwards Chief Justice of the United States, rose and said, "This information is not certain, but there is too much reason to believe it true. After receiving intelligence of a national calamity so heavy and afflicting, the House of Representatives can be but ill-fitted for public business." He then moved an adjournment, and both houses adjourned until the next day. When they again met, Mr. Marshall proposed several resolutions; one of which was, "Resolved, That a committee, in conjunction with one from the Senate, be appointed, to consider on the most suitable manner of paying honour to the memory of the man, first in war, first in peace, and first in the hearts of his fellow-citizens."

The Senate addressed a letter to the President, in

which they said, " Permit us, sir, to mingle our tears with yours.   On this occasion it is manly to weep. To lose such a man, at such a crisis, is no common calamity to the world.   Our country mourns a father.   The Almighty disposer of human events has taken from us our greatest benefactor and orna- ment.   It becomes us to submit with reverence to him ' who maketh darkness his pavilion.' "   The President returned an answer expressive of his sor- row, and. in conclusion, said, " His example is now complete ; and it will teach wisdom and virtue to magistrates, citizens and men ; and not only in the present age, but in future generations, as long as our history shall be read."

So ends the history of the life of that man whom God raised up to be the father of this great nation, and to be an example for all men in authority through out every age.

CHAPTER XVI.

HE two most wonderful persons of the last age—two of the most wonderful men who have lived in the world— were WASHINGTON and NAPOLEON. Our young readers may be presumed to be familiar with the histories of both, and it will not be unprofitable to impress upon their minds their characteristics, separately and in contrast. We shall therefore feel no hesitation in laying before them the fine comparison which follows, by the Hon. James K. Paulding, deeming it the best and simplest that has ever been written.

"The superiority of virtue over mere genius," remarks this author, "was probably never exemplified on a scale of greater magnificence, or more completely demonstrated, than in the lives and fortunes of these two illustrious persons. As a man of genius Napoleon was without doubt superior to Washington, but his virtues bore no comparison to those of the other. In the activity and comprehensiveness of his mind; in that clearness of perception which enabled him to foresee and overcome the obstacles which impeded his course, and achieve an unparalleled succession of triumphs, few men, either of ancient or modern times, equalled him. In these respects, Washington was not his peer perhaps; and yet, when we consider the relative positions of the two, I am inclined to believe he was not much his inferior. He certainly excelled him in wisdom, though he may have been his inferior in genius.

"The mind of Washington was equal to the full and entire comprehension of the sphere in which he acted; and his sagacity in pointing out the probable events of the future, as well as guarding against either present or remote contingencies, is everywhere strikingly displayed, not only in his acts but opinions. His letters to Congress, during the progress of the Revolution, are principally occupied with pointing out approaching danger, or recommending the best means of avoiding it; and it cannot be doubted, that had his advice and exhortations been properly attended to, the struggle for liberty would have been far less protracted and sanguinary. But he was not. like Napoleon, an absolute monarch or leader, the master of his people. He was the servant of his countrymen, and could advise, but not direct nor control their actions or opinions, except by the force of his reasoning and the weight of his character. These constituted almost the only authority he exercised, except in his military capacity; and thus situated, his means were never in any degree correspondent with the greatness of his designs, or the difficulties which beset him at every moment of his military career. We are not, therefore, to judge of his talents by the victories he gained, but by the defeats which he avoided; and his crowning merit as a warrior is, that of having performed great things with weak instruments and comparatively insignificant means.

" Napoleon, on the contrary, in the more early stages of his career, was the absolute leader of an infuriated multitude; a nation of thirty millions of people, acting under the influence of an enthusiasm of which the world furnishes few examples, as to its extent or its consequences. This alone had previously, under leaders of far inferior capacity, achieved a succession of victories over the veteran troops of Europe. Napoleon placed himself at the head of an irresistible impulse, which was sufficient in itself to carry him to the summit of glory. As emperor, he reaped the benefits of this national en thusiasm, which had resulted in the formation of a warlike nation and armies inured to victory, as well as rendered all but invincible by an ardour almost equal to enthusiasm, a confidence the result of a long series of successes amounting to prodigies. With such instruments, aided by the possession of absolute power over a rich and mighty people, it was comparatively easy to conquer nations, governed by enfeebled monarchs reigning over subjects rendered unwarlike by having for centuries relied on standing armies for protection, and disaffected or indifferent toward a government of which they experienced little but the oppressions. But had he been placed in the situation of Washington, equally circumscribed in his means and his authority, there is every reason to believe that for want of the virtues of that pure and illustrious man, rather than from any inferiority of genius, he would have failed in accomplishing the great object of freeing his own country, or subjecting others.

" Napoleon was inferior to Washington in patriotism. He was not born in France ; it was not his native land, endeared to him by the ties and associations of childhood. He loved glory better than France, and sacrificed his adopted country on the altar of insatiable ambition. Without doubt, the position he occupied often entailed on him the necessity of warring in self-defence, even when he seemed the aggressor. It was indispensable that he should be Cæsar or nothing; to overturn the thrones of others, or cease to reign himself. In this point of view, they may be called defensive wars, partaking in the sentiment of patriotism, because the glory and safety of France were identified with his own. But these motives, however they might have mingled incidentally with other more powerful incitements, cannot justify his conduct toward Spain, or his invasion of Russia. His throne was too well established at these times to fear either one or the other; and an impartial posterity, while it pardons many of his apparent aggressions, will, in all probability, denounce these as the offspring not of patriotism but of a boundless ambition, incapable of being satiated by the acquisition of glory or power.

" If we turn toward Washington, we shall see at a glance that ambition, if it at all influenced his acceptance of the command of armies which scarcely had an existence at the time, was only a latent motive, that, of itself alone, could not have stimulated him to assume a station which presented in perspective a very remote and doubtful triumph on one hand, an ignominious death on the other. He was undoubtedly fully aware of the obstacles, difficulties and discouragements which presented themselves on every hand; of the power of the invader and the weakness of his opposers. That he accepted this arduous and discouraging command with doubt and hesitation is apparent from the letter he wrote to Mrs. Washington, announcing that event, as well as the testimony of his nearest connections, whom he either consulted, or who witnessed his struggles. The love of his country, and a sense of her wrongs, were, without doubt, the great, if not the sole motives which induced him to take on his shoulders a burthen perhaps as great as ever man bore, and to persevere in bearing it in the midst of disappointment and defeat, joined to unmerited censure and national ingratitude. That the desire of gain did not in the least influence his decision is apparent, from his stipulating that he should receive nothing for his services but the remuneration of his actual expenditures; and that the love of power was equally absent from his mind, is demonstrated by its resignation the moment his country was free.

" The ambition of Washington was a virtue, that of Napoleon a vice. The limits of the one was the freedom and independence of his country; that of the other the subjugation of a world. One struggled for the rights of his countrymen; the c .her aimed at prostrating the rights of nations. One freed, the other enslaved his country. Finally, Washington drove the enemy from his native soil, while Napoleon eventually drew his enemies into the heart of France, to subjugate her capital, levy contributions, and re-instate on the throne the very family whose misgo-vernment had involved her in so many calamities.

" In dignity of mind; in patience under privation; in fortitude under calamity and disappointment; in forbearance under provocation; in self-possession under misfortune, and moderation in success, Wash-ington was far above Napoleon, who knew how to command others but not himself. The finest feature in the composition of Washington, and that which gives him a superiority over all other characters in history, was that equal and harmonious combination of qualities which distinguished both his head and his heart. They formed a consummate whole; a perfect edifice, every part of which corresponded with the other, and the apparent greatness of which is diminished in the contemplation of its symmetry. Instead of having our admiration attracted to any one particular point, or our wonder excited by some monstrous disproportion, the mind dwells with a delightful complacency on the perfect whole, as the eye rests on the calm beauties of a summer sunset, when nature combines all her harmonies in one, and exhibits at a single view her greatness and her beauty. There was no master-passion in his mind, swallowing up or overshadowing all the rest; and in his virtues there was nothing excessive. We see no camel's hump in the formation of his mind; no disproportioned projection producing wonder without exciting admiration. Like the star of the mariner, he was always the same; always shining bright and clear without dazzling the eye; always pointing one way, "true as the needle to the pole."

"Nor do I believe that, on a closer examination, his military genius will suffer much in comparing it with that of Napoleon. To combine and direct small means to the successful attainment of great ends, is, in my opinion, evidence of greater skill than is exhibited in the conduct of vast enterprises with means fully adequate to the object. The direction of a small, ill-provided, undisciplined, and discontented army, dispirited by past disasters, and anticipating others to come, is certainly not less difficult than leading a well-constituted force, provided with everything necessary, and flushed with victory, to new conquests. In one case, patience fortitude, forbearance, perseverance, an insight into

human motives and passions, and a consummate
skill in their management, is indispensable; in the
other, the machine may be said to govern itself, and
perform its evolutions by the innate force of its own
principles of action. All critics in the art of war
unite in placing the difficulties of conducting a defensive war far above those of an offensive one, and
giving the preference, not to the general who gains
the victory, which is often a mere affair of accident,
but to him who maintains a successful defence
against a superior force, and preserves his army in
the midst of disaster and defeat. I know not among
all the great actions of Napoleon one displaying
greater intrepidity, enterprise and skill, than was
exhibited by Washington at the successive battles
of Trenton and Princeton; and if we are to estimate
their importance by their consequences, the most
celebrated conflicts of ancient and modern times,
where hundreds of thousands were engaged, and
tens of thousands fell, become insignificant in the
comparison. History records that these bloody
and tremendous contests produced for the most part
no permanent results. The possession of a town
or, at most, the temporary occupation of a portion
of the country, was all that was acquired in exchange
for the sacrifice of hecatombs; and even when vic-

tory led to the conquest of states, experience has generally shown that the final result was a restoration of the spoil to its ancient proprietors, or another change of masters in the person of some new conqueror. But these victories of Washington, though gained by small numbers, over numbers not much greater, were followed by consequences at this moment far more momentous than all those of Napoleon combined. They laid a foundation for the successful termination of a struggle which gave liberty to a new world, and whose principles are now at work to achieve a similar triumph in the old The victories of Napoleon have all ended in merely transferring France from the dynasty of Bourbon to that of Orleans.

"Still, the unsullied glory of Washington must ever rest more on his virtues than on his genius; and it is for this reason he has now become, and will remain, so long as the records or traditions of past times are preserved, one of the bright, if not the brightest light of future ages; the safest and noblest example for imitation; the model of a patriot; the incarnation of the spirit of a republican hero. In his life and actions, both in public and private, we see the triumph of virtue, and what wonders she can accomplish. It is there most clearly demonstrated

o

.hat it is not alone to the qualities of the head that men are indebted for the brightest honours, the most imperishable fame, but that those of the heart have a still higher claim to the admiration of mankind. In his person, virtue may be said to have resumed her lawful supremacy, and the example cannot but have the most salutary effects, by giving to public admiration a proper direction, and to public gratitude the noblest object of devotion. In most other heroes the splendour of their achievements throws all their defects and vices into the shade ; but had not Washington been finally successful, he would have stood where he stands now, with only this difference, that instead of being the deliverer, he would have been equally venerated as the great martyr of his country.

"The fate of these two great men of modern times has been as different as was the constitution of their minds. One was crushed under the vast fabric of ambition he had reared on the necks of millions, and cemented with their blood ; the other rose to the highest pinnacle of glory, by limiting his ambition to giving liberty to his country. He did not, like Napoleon, after quelling foreign enemies, turn his sword on her bosom, and become a still more deadly foe by enslaving her himself. The moment of his greatest triumph was when, instead of fomenting the discontents of an army which, under his auspices, had freed the country, and making it the instrument of riveting her chains, he sternly rebuked the incendiaries who had incited it almost to mutiny, and, by the authority of his name and his virtues, at once crushed the meditated treason. The second great triumph was when, having finished the war and secured the liberties he had so long toiled to attain, he surrendered his sword to the President of Congress, at Annapolis. The third and last was, when, after eight years of labour as chief magistrate, in maturing the infant government, establishing its foreign and internal policy, and, in a great measure, perfecting its practical operation, he finally, while still in possession of all his faculties, and of the love and veneration of his country, retired from public life, and at one and the same moment gave to his successors an example of sublime moderation, to his fellow-citizens one of the noblest lessons of political wisdom that ever emanated from the pen of mortal man. What a contrast to the fate of Napoleon, who was unquestionably among the greatest of men, and who wanted nothing to make him perhaps the greatest the world ever saw, but the virtues of Washington!

" Without doubt the different spheres of action in

which these two illustrious men respectively moved
may have had a material influence on their character
and conduct. Both undoubtedly frequently acted
under the pressure of impelling circumstances, or
strong necessity. I do not, therefore, join in echo-
ing the indiscriminate censures heaped on the head
of Napoleon by that bitter, unscrupulous, and unre-
lenting spirit which is characteristic of the British
press. During the latter years of his life he was
contending with England for the empire of the Old
World, as is now sufficiently demonstrated in the
preponderance assumed by that power since his
downfall, and in such a struggle there is no other
alternative than the submission or annihilation of
one or other of the parties. What therefore appears
to us the frenzy of unchastened ambition, may have
been nothing more than self-defence, which is sometimes, nay often, compelled to assume an offensive
attitude of prevention. It is not always that the
invader is the aggressor; and it is at all times per-
fectly justifiable to anticipate a blow we see coming,
by striking the adversary beforehand. Nor do I
wish to elevate Washington at the expense of
another. He cannot shine brighter by the force of
contrast or through any invidious comparisons. He
is among the greatest of men. because he possessed

the greatest virtues, and was blessed by Providence with a vast and comprehensive sphere for their exercise. With him the Temple of Fame is the Temple of Virtue.

"The grand structure sought to be reared by Napoleon has fallen and buried that mighty mortal under its ruins. He attempted to push the world aside from its course, and succeeded for a time. But the bow seems to have been bent the wrong way, and finally broke, or recoiled on himself. His actions were splendid almost beyond comparison, and his genius equally grand. But I apprehend there was some great fundamental error in the course of his career, and cannot help suspecting it was in not giving liberty to France. It would seem that nothing can permanently flourish which is founded in a radical principle of wrong. Kingdoms may be conquered, nations trodden under foot, and for a brief period it may seem that force is triumphant over right; but there is a worm in the chaplet of glory acquired by such means, which will soon cause it to wither and die. There is a natural, irresistible tendency in everything deranged by violence to come in its right place again, either by a speedy reaction, or by going round in a circle, and ending where it began. It would seem that truth alone is everlasting, and that nothing can permanently endure which is founded in wrong or hostile to virtue.

" The career of Napoleon ended in hopeless exile, on a barren rock in the lone and melancholy ocean; that of Washington closed in more than meridian splendour, amid the blessings of his country and the increasing admiration of the world. One left behind him little else than the wrecks of his career; the other founded a vast confederation, every day increasing in space, in numbers and prosperity, and which will continue to do so, only just in proportion as it adheres to his maxims and imitates his example. Napoleon was a bright but scorching luminary, scourging the earth with consuming fires; Washington a genial sun, mild yet radiant; enlightening without dazzling; warming without consuming. Both exhibit great moral lessons to the contemplation of mankind; one as a solemn warning, the other as a glorious example.

" They were emphatically the two great men of the age, and naturally come into comparison with each other, not only on that score, but because, singular as it may seem, they both greatly contributed to the liberties of mankind; one directly, by building up a magnificent edifice of Freedom in

the New World; the other incidentally, by pros
trating the ancient fabrics of despotism in the Old
and demonstrating the utter weakness of kings
when unsupported by the confidence and affections
of the people."

CHAPTER XVII.

BEFORE concluding this volume, it may not be inappropriate to notice the tomb and sarcophagus in which the mortal remains of Washington now rest. The new tomb at Mount Vernon was constructed about ten years ago, upon the site pointed out and especially selected by Washington himself, as mentioned in a preceding chapter of this work. "The will of this great man," says Mr. Strickland, in his 'Tomb of Washington,' "with reference to the removal of the old family vault, has been most scrupulously complied with, through the agency of his then only surviving executor, Major Lawrence Lewis, the nephew and friend of the illustrious deceased.

"This structure consists simply of an excavation made partly in the side of a steep, sloping hill, which has a southern exposure upon a thickly-wooded dell. The walls are built of brick, and arched over at the

neight of eight feet above the level of the ground.
The front of the tomb-house is roughcast, and has a
plain iron door, inserted in a strong freestone case-
ment; over the door is placed a sculptured stone
panel, upon which are inscribed these impressive
words:

> "I AM THE RESURRECTION AND THE LIFE; HE
> THAT BELIEVETH IN ME, THOUGH HE
> WERE DEAD, YET SHALL HE LIVE."

At a small distance from the walls of the tomb,
on all sides, there is a surrounding enclosure of
brick-work, elevated to a height of twelve feet, and
guarded in front with an iron gateway, opening
several feet in advance of the vault door. This
gateway is flanked with pilasters, surmounted by a
stone cornice and coping, covering a pointed gothic
arch, over which is sculptured, upon a plain slab,
inserted in the brick-work:

> "WITHIN THIS ENCLOSURE REST THE REMAINS
> OF GENERAL GEORGE WASHINGTON."

The sarcophagus, which now incloses the sacred
dust of the Great Founder, owes its origin to the
patriotism and public spirit of a mechanic of Philadelphia. Early in 1837, Major Lewis, surviving
executor of Washington's will, applied to John

Struthers, marble mason, as he styles himself, sculptor we shall always call him, to execute a suitable marble coffin to inclose these interesting remains. In answer to this application, Mr. Struthers requested permission to execute, at his own cost, a sarcophagus, which he hoped might be deemed worthy of so honourable a distinction. This permission was cheerfully accorded; and in August of the same year the work was completed. In order to direct the suitable manner of placing the sarcophagus, and to witness the removal of the remains, Mr. Struthers, accompanied by his friend Mr. Strickland, went to Mount Vernon, early in October.

The following touching account of the removal of Washington's remains to their final resting place, is extracted from Mr. Strickland's account of this visit, contained in his elegant volume entitled "The Tomb of Washington."

"On the morning of the 7th we repaired to Mount Vernon, and found the Sarcophagus had arrived, and was deposited in front of the enclosure; and the workmen, assisted by a few of the domestics belonging to the household, were directed to dig out a suitable foundation upon which to wall up and place it, on the *right* of the entrance gate. During the operation the steward was directed to procure lights for the purpose of entering the vault, and preparing the way for the removal of the body to the outside of the vault. The gate of the enclosure was temporarily closed, and upon the opening of the vault door we entered, accompanied by Major Lewis and his son. The coffin containing the remains of Washington was in the extreme back part of the vault; and to remove the case containing the leaden receptacle, it was found necessary to put aside the coffins that were piled up between it and the doorway. After clearing a passage-way, the case, which was much decayed, was stripped off, and the lead of the lid was discovered to have sunk very considerably from head to foot; so much so, as to form a curved line of four to five inches in its whole length. This settlement of the metal had perhaps caused the soldering of the joints to give way about the upper or widest part of the coffin. At the request of Major Lewis this fractured part was turned over on the lower part of the lid, exposing to view a head and breast of large dimensions, which appeared, by the dim light of the candles, to have suffered but little from the effects of time. The eye-sockets were large and deep, and the breadth across the temples. together with the forehead, appeared of unusual size There was no appearance of grave-clothes; the chest was broad; the colour was dark, and had the appearance of dried flesh and skin adhering closely to the bones. We saw no hair, nor was there any offensive odour from the body, but we observed, when the coffin had been removed to the outside of the vault, the dripping down of a yellow liquid, which stained the marble of the Sarcophagus. A hand was laid upon the head and instantly removed; the lead of the lid was restored to its place; the body, raised by six men, was carried and laid in the marble coffin, and the ponderous cover being put on and set in cement, it was sealed from our sight on Saturday, the 7th day of October, 1837."

The following description of the top and side views of the Sarcophagus, are copied from the same volume.

"The construction of the Sarcophagus is of the modern form, and consists of an excavation from a solid block of marble, eight feet in length, three feet in width, and two feet in height, resting on a plinth, which projects four inches round the base of the coffin. The lid or covering stone is a ponderous block of Italian marble, emblazoned with the arms and insignia of the United States, beautifully sculp-tured in the boldest relief. The design occupies a arge portion of the central part of the top surface,

or lid, and represents a shield, divided into thirteen perpendicular stripes, which rests on the flag of our country, and is attached by cords to a spear, embellished with tassels, forming a background to the shield, by which it is supported. The crest is an eagle with open wings, perching upon the superior bar of the shield, and in the act of clutching the arrows and olive branch. Between these armorial

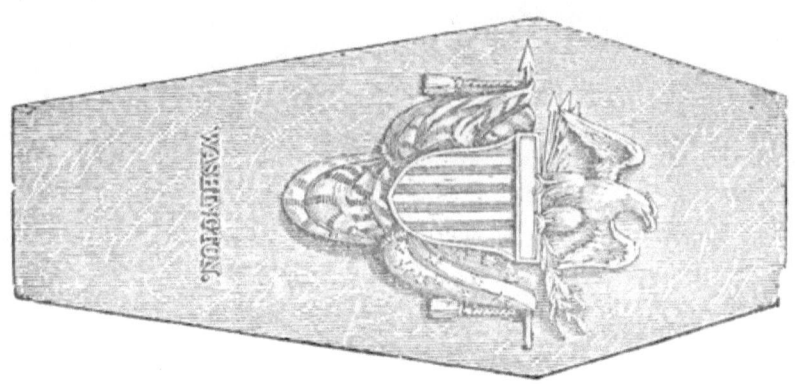

bearings and the foot of the coffin, upon the plain field of the lid, is the bold and deeply sculptured name of

"WASHINGTON."

" The foot of the coffin is inscribed as follows:

"BY THE PERMISSION OF LAWRENCE LEWIS, ESQ.,
THIS SARCOPHAGUS OF WASHINGTON WAS
PRESENTED BY JOHN STRUTHERS, OF
PHILADELPHIA, MARBLE MASON."

The remains of Mrs. Washington are now deposited in a marble coffin, sculptured in a plain manner by the same chisel, and occupy the space on the *left* of the gateway, or entrance to the tomb.

THE END.

LEE AND SHEPARD'S BOOKS OF TRAVEL.